Summoned

Aella C Grey

About the Book:

"Religion is a war, Oriana, and love will be the only way we reach salvation."

Oriana Sharpe is your average student at the esteemed Divine Covenant College, but her journey to become a trauma counselor takes a turn when what she thought was an innocent and fake spell cast by her best friend Rae leaves her haunted by a mysterious voice.

As she grapples with her sudden onset of psychosis, she's attacked by her religious studies professor Mr. Merrick, but what she doesn't expect is for this mysterious voice to help her.

Her world takes another unexpected turn when she learns that the voice that helped her has a name, and maybe even a body.

With Mr. Merrick still alive and her safety in jeopardy, Oriana must navigate a path where allies are few and trust is elusive, in a world where the boundaries of good and evil blur.

She must decide whether her aspirations are worth the cost of her life, and maybe even her soul.

Will Oriana succumb to demons, or will love conquer?

Find out in this standalone paranormal romance novel, and the first book in the Prince of Hell series.

The Author:

Aella C Grey is an author hailing from Winnipeg, MB, Canada, currently residing in the sunny state of Florida. When she's not immersed in the world of writing, Aella indulges in her other passions, such as playing video games, diving into captivating books, and cherishing quality time with her beloved dog and supportive husband.

With a vivid imagination and a deep appreciation for storytelling, Aella brings her unique perspective to the realm of fiction. Her love for literature and interactive entertainment has fueled her creative endeavors, inspiring her to craft compelling narratives that transport readers to captivating worlds.

Aella's writing draws readers in with dynamic characters, intriguing plots, and a touch of magic. Whether she's exploring mystical realms or delving into the complexities of the human experience, her stories are infused with emotion, suspense, and a dash of the unexpected.

Stay connected with Aella C. Grey through her website to discover more about her upcoming works, behind-the-scenes insights, and to join her on thrilling literary adventures.

Summoned

Prince of Hell I

by

Aella C Grey

1. Edition, 2025

Table of Contents

Important

Much like the Unbroken, the Prince of Hell series has ties to real world problems, which some readers may find uncomfortable. As with all fictional books, the relationships are special in their own way, with characters that have their own personalities and flaws. None of my writing is meant to diminish the seriousness of what individuals have gone through in their lives, nor is my writing meant to demean religion in any way, shape or form.

Trigger warnings:

Anxiety, Alcohol, Attempted Assault, Attempted Rape, Blood, Bullying, Child Abuse, Cults, Death, Demons, Drug Use, Eating Disorder, Gore, Hospitalization, Kidnapping, Murder, Mental Health Crisis, Needles, Profanity, Religion, Religious Trauma, Secret Society, Sexually Explicit Scenes, Violence

Glossary

There are multiple pronunciations for these words, especially given different dialects, so please see the phonetic pronunciation below as intended for this series.

Seir (See-er), Oriana (Oh-ree-ah-nuh), Rae (Ray)
Arrenault (Arr-eh-n-alt), Merrick (Meh-rr-ick)
Vassago (Vah-sah-go), Greenberg (Gree-n-berg)
Daimōn (Dey-mohn), Godfrey (God-free), Barclay (Bar-clay)
Marianne (Mah-ree-ann), Janine (Jah-nee-n), Abbess (Ah-bess)
Qur'an (Qur-ahn), Ramayana (Rah-mah-yuh-nuh)
Mahabharata (Ma-hab-hara-ta), Puranas (Pu-rah-nuh)
Upanishads (Oo-pan-i-shads)
Bhagavad Gita (Buh-guh-vuh-d gee-ta)
Lemegeton (Le-meh-jeh-ton), Solomon (Sol-uh-muhn)
Grimoire (Grim-wah-r), Goetia (Go-eh-sha)
Theurgia (Thee-ur-jee-ah), Paulina (Paw-lee-nah)
Almadel (All-mah-del), Notoria (No-toh-ree-ah)
Bael (Bay-ehl), Asmodeus (Az-moe-dee-us), Purson (Per-son)
Vine (Vy-n), Beleth (Buh-leth), Paimon (Pay-mon)
Balam (Ba-lahm), Zagan (Zai-g-ahn), Belial (Bee-lie-all)
Agares (Ay-gar-es), Dantalion (Dan-tal-eon)
Amdusias (Am-do-see-as), Vapula (Vah-pool-ah)
Aym (Ay-m), Bathin (Bah-th-een), Zepar (Zeh-par)
Eligos (E-lee-gos), Gusion (Gu-sh-ion), Barbas (Bahr-bahs)
Valefor (Val-eh-four), Vepar (Veh-par), Astaroth (As-tuh-roth)
Berth (Behr-ith), and Buné (Boo-neh) Ipos (Eye-poh-s)
Sitri (Sih-t-ree), Gäap (Guh-ahp), Stolas (Sto-l-ahs)
Orobas (Oh-roh-bas)

To all those who have felt like a burden, who felt like the
world was against them at every turn...
This one is for you.

Prologue

"Please momma, can I have that one?"

Her honey-brown eyes widen and her sandy skin turns a tinge of pink as I tug on her hand, pointing at the poster on the side of the ice cream shop.

Chocolate chip cookie dough is my favorite. Momma knows it's my favorite. We haven't had ice cream in so long.

"Momma," I tug again once as her rose-tinted lips pull into a thin line. "We never get ice cream anymore. Why?"

Her face turns more red, and I know that means I need to quiet down, but now I'm upset. I'm more upset at how we never get ice cream any more than I am about not having ice cream right now.

"Momma, I want ice cream."

The whine in my voice catches the attention of nearby pedestrians, and within seconds momma starts to walk away from the store, pulling me along behind her at a brisk pace that nearly has me stumbling over my own toes to keep up.

She's squeezing my hand so tight that I wince and try to pull my hand from hers. "Momma!"

She whirls around, bringing her face an inch from mine as her mouth pulls into a low snarl. "Stop it, Oriana. Stop it right now. I don't know what evil possesses you, child, but no daughter of mine will show this much greed."

Tears well in my eyes as I stare at the anger etched into her features.

Maybe if I can just tell her why I want to get ice cream, she won't be so angry.

"Momma, I—"

"Enough, Oriana!" She whirls back around and drags me along behind her, not caring when I stumble, and she has to hoist me up by my arm to stand me upright again.

Pain lances through my shoulder, but I stay quiet, sniffling as snot runs from my nose, mixing with the tears at my chin. We finally see the car up ahead, and I fixate on it, knowing that soon I'll be able to sit in the back seat alone where I won't bother them.

I don't want to bug momma and papa.

They seem so much happier together when I'm quiet.

The tip of my shoe catches on a jagged edge of the pavement, and I tumble forward just as she yanks her arm upright. A sudden tearing feeling in my shoulder has me gasp before sharp pain radiates through my arm and I cry out. The shrill sound has momma's head jerk toward me, but she glances around before she continues toward the vehicle.

"Momma, stop!" My cries are pleading but she won't listen. Something is wrong.

I don't understand. Why is she so mad at me? What did I do?

She tugs again as my pace slows down, and I scream at the white-hot pain that lances down to my elbow.

"Shut up, Oriana. Stop making a scene because of ice cream. You greedy, vile, devilish child."

How can I tell her it hurts? She's already so mad at me.

The driver's side door opens, and papa takes one look at me with a guarded expression before glancing at the other people on the street.

"What happened?"

My breath catches and I hiccup as I open my mouth to tell him my arm hurts, but momma opens the passenger door angrily.

"She needs another treatment. This time, tell Father Arrenault to get the demons out of her, or I will do it myself."

Papa sighs, giving me a look that makes me want to sink into a deep hole and never come out.

He's disappointed.

Tears well in my eyes some more, and momma shoves me toward the car roughly.

Why are they so mad? Is this all because I asked for ice cream?

You greedy, vile, devilish child.

I hardly pull my arms into the seat fully when the door slams shut, and I slowly tug the seatbelt over my chest with a wince. My right arm tingles, and I gingerly touch it, feeling that same sensation like when you sit for too long and your legs go numb.

Papa gets into the car first, and I see his eyes lock onto me in the mirror.

"Papa," I whisper, hoping that my voice doesn't upset him. "My arm hurts."

He glances at where my hand covers my shoulder, but when momma opens the other door, I quickly look away to watch people passing by. Papa sighs again, and the engine rumbles to life as he pulls onto the main road.

"She needs to learn manners, and find God again." Momma murmurs, her voice still exasperated as papa nods.

"I'll take her to see Father Arrenault in Rennensberg tomorrow."

My heart drops into my stomach remembering past treatments they sent me for. Father Arrenault seems far younger than momma and papa, but he's mean. They made me stay at his camp for kids. There's so many chores to do there, and even if you're tired you can't say anything, or you'll be punished for laziness.

He wouldn't feed me unless I obeyed.

No water unless I obeyed.

No going home, unless I obeyed.

Weeks of treatment where I'd be broken down to nothing but a shell of myself.

I'm never asking for anything ever again.

- 5 -

Chapter 1

Years later....

"Oooo, what about this one? It's a *love* spell!"

I glance over to where Rae is, pointing at the screen of her laptop with a smile spread across her face like she just unlocked the secret to the universe.

Rolling my eyes, I flop to my side, and rest my palm against my cheek. "That would be great if any of the guys at school were worth the miniscule amount of time we have left in the world."

She frowns, fixing me with a deadpan green-eyed stare. "Well aren't you a bundle of sunshine today."

I bite my tongue as a moment of tense silence passes between us, and she sighs loudly. "Fuck. I'm sorry, Ori. I shouldn't have been so insensitive."

I stay quiet, nodding slightly with my eyes glued to the ceiling, and she types some more on her laptop.

It's only been two months since the freak car accident that took my parents' lives, and somehow, after a week of it being everywhere on Gracefield's local news, everyone seemed to continue on like nothing happened. Once the funeral ended, I moved in to my godparent's second townhouse near campus with their daughter, who also happens to be my life-long best friend.

We go to the same college, and attend some of the same classes. I'm working toward getting a degree in Religious Studies so that I can become a counselor for those healing from the traumas that can come with a life saturated in religion. I only truly saw it for what it was when I was sixteen, and by then I'd already been exposed to so much. It wasn't until the bitter end that I realized how bad it had been.

My parents devoted their entire lives to the church here in Gracefield, only to have everything ripped from them. Even my childhood home ended up being donated to Divine Covenant per their will.

The knowledge that they donated it instead of leaving it to me stung, but that house held my best and worst memories. Moments of a loving family overshadowed by the painful realization that they only loved me, only poured happiness into me when it benefited their status with Him and the church. Their affection was conditional whereas mine wasn't. Growing up, they would sooner tell me that God loves me than saying it themselves, and any time I fell short of their expectations, I was a disappointment.

Between the inner turmoil of rejecting from their beliefs, and the accompanying threats of going to hell, accusations of being the devil, impending eternal punishments and the like...

All of it made me want to be there for people who got out.

For people healing like I am.

Rae, on the other hand, is going to school to become a lawyer, so we share a handful of classes, but not all of them. It hasn't been so bad. We go to school together, come home together, hang out after class together.

It's just felt like one of those sleepovers where you stay so long that you're beyond ready to go home.

Except, I have no other home to go to.

I have no home, no remaining family outside of Rae and my godparents. I have never felt more like an outsider than I do now.

Four years ago, if you had asked me during my freshman year what the loneliest feeling was, I'd have said it was going to high school for the first time.

Now? Now I can confidently say that it's every day of this living, breathing, waking nightmare.

In my peripherals Rae glances at me hesitantly, and I know she's about to try to change the subject.

"Ha, this one says we need to say these words three times in front of a mirror for the spell to work, but we would get eternal beauty."

Bingo.

As if any of these 'spells' are real anyways. They're all just random posts people put on the internet for views.

I guess playing the game won't hurt.

Raising a brow at her, I tilt my head and force a smile. "Are we supposed to say Bloody Mary three times? Because I'm pretty sure there's no eternal beauty that comes from that one."

She laughs, and though I feel myself smiling back at her, I can't help the emptiness I feel inside. This void within me has made it hard enough to eat and sleep, let alone feel any happiness, or joy.

Rae scrolls a bit more and pauses, slamming her hand down excitedly onto the carpet. "This is the one, Ori! 'Unlock a hidden superpower,' that sounds like something we'd want!"

She scrambles to her closet, and I blink at her as she digs around through the jar in the corner. It's packed full of random things we've collected over the past few weeks since we'd started this obsession with witchcraft.

My brows pinch together as she places a feather, some random stones and a couple odds and ends beside her before sitting back on her heel with a satisfied sigh.

"Okay, now we just need blood."

My eyes widen. "You're joking."

Rae shakes her head, and her brown, shoulder-length hair shifts side to side with the movement. "Nope, but it doesn't say how much, so I'm thinking a drop will do."

She scoops the collection of items into her palms and scurries over, plopping them in front of me before leaning toward the corner of the bed, reaching between the mattresses and pulling out a blade.

I wince, staring at the sharp blade in her hands. "Rae, do I even wanna know why you have a pocket knife under your bed?"

She blinks at it, her features fully innocent as she meets my gaze. "Well... I mean... I always keep one at each end, just in case of emergencies." Reaching between us, she places the feather and other items into a shallow bowl before snatching my hand.

"What—? Wait, why am I the guinea pig?"

She just laughs. "Because between the two of us, I think you're less likely to spontaneously combust if suddenly given superpowers."

The blade digs into my skin, and just as the sharp pain registers in my fingertip, she pulls back, squeezing my finger as a drop of blood falls into the bowl.

I frown, watching as she mixes the items and places them into a small jar. "Aren't you supposed to say something?"

She secures a cork on top before snagging the purple candle beside her with a shrug. "I dunno, this is just what the website said to do. We didn't have some of the exact items though, so I substituted them. Like it said to use an eagle feather, but we only have a crow's. Nothing crazy different. I'm sure it's all the same though."

Great, we're not only casting spells but improvising.

The flick of her lighter sounds out, and the area between us glows as the candle wick catches with a small stream of smoke.

What if this works? There's no way this could actually happen, right?

The first drop of violet wax drips onto the cork of the jar, followed by another, and with each subsequent drop, my anxiety rises.

Will I know? Is it instant?

By now, the entire cork is covered in purple wax that's hardened as it slowly drips down the sides.

Honestly, I have to admit it looks kinda cool.

"Well?"

My eyes snap to Rae's as she stares at me expectantly. "Well, what?"

She huffs in feigned annoyance. "Well, try to do something! Let's see what powers you got!"

"You can't seriously think that jar gave me superpowers."

A sudden flash of light in the window catches my eye before the power flickers off, and Rae shrieks as thunder booms outside the house. I can barely see her arms covering her head protectively in the dim light from the window.

"Stop, Ori! I don't want to die!"

Grabbing her arm, I give it a tug. "Rae, stop. That's not funny. It wasn't me."

The moment she raises her head, a bang sounds from downstairs and we both jump, staring at one another with wide eyes in the dark room.

Her arm trembles in my grip as her nervous voice fills the air. "Should we...?"

Conflicted between being the typical person in every horror movie who dies first, and the smart one, I nod. "Yeah, let's go check it out."

We're halfway down the stairs when her mom's voice calls from the kitchen, "Girls?"

Relief washes over me like a warm blanket as I release a tense breath. Rae's parents tend to stop by sometimes with food, and our fridge was looking scarce. So while this is unexpected, it's for the best.

At least it wasn't me. The last thing I'd want is to burn Rae's house down.

My mind wanders to my childhood home, and I swallow the bitterness down.

Come to think of it, that's a house that could use some remodeling.

Quiet laughter rings out from beside me, and I turn to see Rae at the top of the stairs, waving for me to follow her.

Her voice is hushed as she whispers, "Hurry! We left everything out, if she sees it, she'll burn us at the stake."

I frown. *It really seemed like she was right beside me.*

Footsteps echo downstairs, and my heart leaps into my throat as I take double steps to the top, hurtling myself into the bedroom. We're both scrambling against time to put everything back into the closet, and we just barely get it closed before throwing ourselves onto the bed as the door slides open.

Rae's mom peers into the room, her short dark hair illuminated by the flash of lightning from the window. "Did you hear me calling you? There's pizza downstairs."

My heart races, and I swallow against the lump in my throat as Rae clears hers. "Uh, no. Sorry mom. We'll be right down."

Didn't hear—my ass.

A huff of barely suppressed laughter sounds out again, and my gaze flicks to Rae, who is now fully cast in darkness on the bed.

"Alright. Hopefully the power will be back on soon. Flashlights will be on the table downstairs."

"Thanks Mrs. Greenberg." My voice cracks as the door slides shut. We listen to her footsteps receding down the stairs, and I swallow audibly as another crack of thunder sounds nearby. "What was so funny earlier?"

There's a moment of silence before the bed shifts, and a flash of lightning illuminates Rae's confused features from the window.

"Funny? I was fighting for my life. I'm so out of shape." She chuckles and scooches closer. "Come on, let's go get some pizza before it gets cold."

An odd feeling of unease sinks into my gut, but I let it go as she pushes off the bed and heads to the door.

I couldn't have been hearing things, could I?

Following close behind Rae to the kitchen, the scent of melted cheese and grease invades my senses. My stomach growls angrily, as if it's been days since I've eaten, and I start to mentally recount my meals over the last week.

Actually, come to think of it, I can't remember the last time I've eaten.

I guess hunger can't be ignored forever. But maybe I could go a little longer?

"Eat."

Chapter 2

The commanding male voice freezes me in place as Rae flips open the box, and I'm half convinced that I imagined it when the voice speaks inside my mind again.

"Starving yourself won't do any good for anyone. Eat."

"Ori?"

With my heart racing, I meet Rae's gaze in the shadows as she takes a bite of food.

"You okay? You look like you've seen a ghost." She grins, still chewing as another flash of lightning brightens the kitchen.

My mouth drops open, and I blink before glancing at the pizza, but I'm at a loss for words.

I have to be imagining this. Either that or my parents death has finally taken its toll.

"Hello? Earth to Ori." Rae waves her free hand in front of my vision.

*"Eat, **Ori**."*

My mouth snaps shut, and I clear my throat awkwardly. "Sorry. Must be my nerves from the storm."

A deep chuckle fills my mind as I move closer to the box and take a slice. Holding it to my mouth, I pause.

Am I really about to do something just because a voice in my head told me to?

*"Yes, I'm your subconscious, telling you to eat something because **someone** has to."*

The sarcasm in his voice is thick, and even though everything in my mind screams that this is just a figment of my imagination, he sounds so real that it's nearly impossible to brush him off.

My heart pounds in my chest as I take a bite of food, chewing slowly while Rae blinks at me.

"I think this is the first time I've seen you eat in days," she says, tilting her head in the dark, before placing her hand on my arm. "Hey, are you okay?"

Fuck no, I'm not okay. Nothing has been okay for months.

"I'm fine. Just tired, I guess. I'm gonna go to sleep early tonight to get a head start in the morning. Mr. Harvard's dog is a handful."

Mr. Harvard is one of our *prestigious* college professors who asked me to walk his dog during one of my free periods. It's a quick way to earn some money since he lives across the street from campus, and all I've ever had to deal with is his dog's shitty behavior about getting his collar on.

Sure, Mr. Harvard is kind of a creep, but he's never been home during the three weeks I've been doing this. He's usually already on campus by the time I get there.

Rae nods, "Okay, just be careful, I don't want to have to drive you to the hospital."

I take another bite of pizza and my stomach churns uneasily before tossing the rest of the slice in the garbage with a shrug. "It's just a flesh wound." I mutter as I walk down the hallway to the spare bedroom.

The voice chuckles again, and my stomach flips nervously. *Great. This is exactly what I needed—an imaginary, bossy voice in my head that laughs at my jokes.*

Maybe I should consider a career more focused in psychology.

Another boom of thunder shakes the house as rain patters against the window. Taking a few steps into the room, I let out a deep-seated sigh.

Sleeping this off should do the trick...
I hope.

Chapter 3

Birds chirp loudly outside the window as my phone's blaring alarm echoes through the room, and I groan. My fingers fumble roughly on the bedside table until I find the screen of my phone.

Swiping the alarm off with more force than intended, the pressure sends my phone clattering to the hardwood floor.

"Fuck."

"Such language."

I sit upright and freeze, my heart suddenly pounding at the voice that is very much out of place in my head. The voice that should have left with a full night's rest.

Okay. Okay don't freak out.

"I hate to be the bearer of bad news, but you are freaking out." It sounds like the voice is smiling; is that even possible?

Shut up.

"Make me. Oh wait."

Ugh.

Grabbing my phone from the ground, I flip it over to see a web of cracks throughout the screen, and my heart sinks.

No, no, no. I just got this!

I swipe my thumb across the screen to unlock it, but nothing registers as the display goes dim again. "Great. Just my luck. First a voice, now my phone. Next up, the end of the world as we know it."

"Well, that's a bit dramatic."

The voice laughs quietly, and the sound echoes through my head as if he's sitting on the bed next to me.

I swallow hard. *Okay, figment of my imagination. Feel free to leave at any time.*

He laughs again before going silent, and I'm not naïve enough to believe this is the end of it, but concern continues to grow in the back of my mind as I consider what the hell this means for me.

Pretty sure there's a diagnosis for people who hear voices.

This has to be some kind of mental break.

At what point do I admit myself into a hospital?

"You're not crazy, Ori."

Says the fucking voice in my head!

Exasperated, I stomp over to the dresser and pull out a dark frilled skirt and blouse. There's no way this is going to disrupt my life more than it already has; this voice is going to have to just sit on the side-lines.

I can ignore it. It's fine. This is fine.

Fresh bacon wafts from the kitchen as I leave the bedroom, and the clatter of dishes fills the air as I grab a towel from the linen closet while Rae's phone alarm rings.

Shit, it's already 9 AM. I'm going to be late.

I scramble into the bathroom, hardly glancing at myself as I tear off my clothes and step into the brisk water streaming from the shower head. The water is barely warmed by the time I finish, and I hurry out to dry off, pulling my clothes over my still-damp skin as my wet hair sticks to my face. Water drips onto my clothes from the tips of my long, dark brown curls as I grab my school bag from the floor of my room and rush out the door.

Snacking on a strip of bacon I grabbed on the way out, I chew slow as I walk the few blocks to Mr. Harvard's house. The autumn air is crisp as I inhale deeply, letting the tension in my body dissipate with each breath which forms a dense cloud of fog.

An odd note of peace feels like it's settled around me, and I find myself zoning out at I walk mindlessly down the street.

At least the voice is gone.

Birds chirp cheerfully from the trees as the sun peeks over the horizon, and I squint as it blinds most of my vision. Taking the last few steps to the empty street still half-blinded, I'm not paying attention, and hardly glance both ways before moving to cross. The moment my foot leaves the ground, the voice in my head booms.

"Ori!"

I take the full step and freeze suddenly, hearing the screech of breaking tires as I snap my head toward the sound. The car swerves, skidding to a halt a few feet in front of me, and my pulse races, flooding my veins with adrenaline.

My chest heaves as if I just sprinted a mile in two and a half seconds, and the passenger's side window rolls down. "Watch where you're walking!" Tires squeal as the middle-aged man drives off, and I roll my eyes.

I don't want to even think about the voice. Nope. Not doing it.

Thankfully it remains quiet the rest of the way there, and by the time I reach Mr. Harvard's enormous property, my nerves are frayed. The large iron gates come into view, and I step up to the electronic pad on the side. The four buttons beep with each press before a long, steady tone signals the code was accepted, and mechanical whirring fills the air as the gate pulls open.

I don't know how this guy affords such a nice property on a college professor's salary. Granted it is a privately funded college and shares funding with Divine Covenant Church, so he's likely well compensated from donors, not to mention the hefty student loans most need to attend.

Barking echoes from inside the house, and my hands tremble from residual nervousness as Jax's silhouette appears behind the frosted glass. I punch in the code on the pad, and a loud beep with a green light signals the door is unlocked.

Twisting the knob open, I squeeze through the crack in the door as Jax's nails clatter against the ground excitedly.

"Hey boy." My voice hardly carries through the hallway as I close the door behind me, and his tail wags back and forth like a whip. I crouch to pet him, running my hand along his fur as he wiggles. "Alright, let's get this over with."

I straighten and venture further into the house. Mr. Harvard usually leaves Jax's collar and leash by the back door, and it's only a few seconds before I turn the corner into the kitchen.

My heart drops as I hear Mr. Harvard's muffled voice nearby.

He shouldn't be here, he's always on campus by now. Did I show up too early?

A loud thud reverberates down the hallway before something distantly clatters to the ground, as if something large was thrown at a wall.

My pulse spikes. I'm about to take another step closer the collar hanging just mere feet away, when the sound of someone whimpering freezes me in place.

The tone sounded pained, but my cheeks flush when I consider it could have been the sound of something intimate.

"Ori, you should leave."

Brilliant idea subconscious. I need to walk this dog.

Another two thuds followed by a fearful, pained cry make my stomach turn, and I'm torn between action and inaction as my heart pounds in my throat.

"Forget the dog. Leave." The urgency in his voice makes me only more anxious.

What if someone needs help?

"You can't help if you're dead." The bluntness of the voice makes me swallow hard, and as footsteps from the hallway grow closer, I'm forced into action if only to pretend I heard nothing.

"Hey, Jax! Time to walk, boy!"

My voice cracks as I step loudly, as if pretending to have just arrived as Mr. Harvard turns the corner. His brown eyes dart around the kitchen, and I don't miss the disheveled look of his dress shirt, the scratch on his jaw, and the tear in his sleeve.

"Oriana?"

He's wiping a cloth between his hands, and it takes a serious effort to avoid glancing down. Even in my peripherals, it's not hard to spot the swelling in his knuckles or the redness of them which only makes my heart pound harder, and adrenaline starts to pump into my veins in earnest.

Fuck.

The voice sighs loudly but I ignore it, doing my best to school my features.

"Oh, hey Mr. Merrick. What are you doing home? Don't you have class?" I frown and tilt my head, hoping to God he sees it as honest, innocent confusion.

"Merrick? What the fuck happened to Mr. Harvard?"

It's a nickname. Now shut up and let me focus—please.

He crosses his arms and narrows his eyes at me as I bend down to pet Jax, if only to distract myself from my nerves.

"Class was canceled today, so I didn't need you to walk Jax. Did you not get my text?"

I grimace and shake my head, "I dropped my phone when my alarm went off this morning, so the screen isn't working."

"That was dumb to admit, Ori."

I know the voice is right.

Not just because my body feels like it could break into a sprint at any moment, but also because Merrick's demeanor shifted as soon as he learned I had no way to contact anyone.

"I can go—"

Merrick puts his palm up and waves it dismissively. "You're already here. Go take him for a walk, and I'll have your cash ready when you get back."

"Oriana..." The voice warns, and I know he wants me to leave, but if I tip Merrick off now, the rest of this school year will be hell.

"Uh, sure." I step toward the collar, my limbs trembling as he sidesteps to intercept me.

"I'll get it for you."

I watch him as he turns, grasping the collar and leash before passing them to me. I can't help but notice how his bruised and split knuckles turn white before he releases the leather leash into my palm.

"Alright," I whisper, taking a healthy step away from Merrick toward the door as Jax follows close behind. "We'll be back in a jiffy."

I'm in a daze as I hook the collar around Jax's neck, keeping my attention focused on the empty hallway from the kitchen. I barely notice his low growl or the way his lips curl in warning as my mind races through what just happened.

"Ori, there's no way you can come back. He knows you know."

What? Am I supposed to just steal his fucking dog?

"I was actually thinking you could release the hound to the wild, but, stealing the mutt could work too."

The thirty-minute walk feels like an eternity, yet also nowhere near long enough as I approach the gates again, keying into the pad before it beeps loudly.

Everything feels wrong. It's like I'm walking into a trap, but I don't know if I'm just overthinking it.

What if I'm assuming and overreacting? Maybe he was just—

"Best case scenario, he was fucking someone and got too rough, Ori. But I've never known knuckles to look like that after sex, have you?"

The voice is annoyingly right again.

Jax tugs on the leash, pulling me toward the dreaded entrance as my heart races so fast that it feels like it might burst from my chest.

Get in, get out.

I twist the knob, letting Jax step inside first as the clatter of his nails shatter the silence through the house. My pulse pounds in my ears as I unclip his leash and carry the small bag of poop to the back door, just like usual. I had considered bringing it home, but it's become a ritual to leave a bag of poop every time.

Even if Merrick isn't home, I don't want to do anything outside of the normal routine.

With each step to the garbage, it feels as if I'm walking the plank—like I'm one step closer to my own end. I drop the bag into the bin and almost sigh in relief when a sudden thud makes me jump as I spin around quickly.

He's standing less than a foot away, his chest heaving as he stares at me with wild eyes.

My voice trembles as I take a hesitant step back. "Mr. Merrick?"

He crouches ever so slightly, and his stance widens. "You shouldn't have been here today."

"Oriana, run. Now!"

I don't let myself think as I dart to the side, sprinting out of the kitchen toward the dining room. With my limited knowledge of the house, I manage to escape down a connecting hall before hitting to a dead end with an empty nook on one side and what looks like a linen closet on the other.

Turning slowly, I see Merrick's tall form in the center of the only exit. His features are painted with a mixture of rage and something else I can't quiet place, but some small part of me dreads that it looks reminiscent of excitement as he steps closer.

"Ori, you need to listen to me very closely."

Merrick takes another step, and I notice the splatter of blood on his shirt which sends a cold wave of panic through my body.

*"**Oriana**."* The voice's urgency cuts through the terror jumbling my mind, pausing my fight-or-flight instincts, if only for a moment.

I'm listening.

He takes another step closer. "I'm sorry it had to be this way, but I can't let you leave... you know this."

I swallow hard, adrenaline pumping through my veins as my limbs tremble.

"You need to let me in, Ori."

My brows furrow, and I take a tentative step back as my heel hits the wall. "You don't have to do this Merrick, I don't know what's going on. I know nothing." He takes another confident step forward with his palms outstretched between us as if I'm a wild animal he's trying to tame.

"Oriana, let me in." The voice's tone is a mix of panic and command, and confusion rifles through me when I finally process what it is requesting.

What do you mean? You're my imagination, you're not real.

"I'm the best fucking chance for your survival right now, but you need to let me in."

Merrick creeps forward slowly like a predator waiting to pounce as the air catches in my lungs. "Even if that were true, Oriana, you know far too much now."

We both lunge at the same time, but I hardly get halfway past Merrick when he grabs my arm painfully, throwing me into the drywall so hard that my skull smashes into it. Stars fill my vision as a fist swings toward my face, and I barely dodge it before his bruising grip on my left arm makes me cry out.

I scream into the silence of the hallway as Jax's clattering nails grow closer. Merrick's hand wraps around my throat as he pins me to the wall, and he searches my face with a maliciousness I've never seen before.

He's really trying to kill me.

"He isn't going to just try, he will. Let me in." The voice is desperate with a hard edge now, and I gasp against the fingers digging into my throat, cutting off my air.

"Oriana!"

Desperation coats my veins as darkness shadows the corners of my vision.

Please. I don't want to die. Help me.

Chapter 4

A bitter, metallic tang coats my mouth as I slowly come to my senses. Pain radiates in my skull, and I slowly recall the moments before blacking out. My eyes peel open to see a body slumped beside me, with crimson pooled on the ground between us.

What the fuck.

My eyes widen, and my mind goes completely blank as I stare in shock at the hardly recognizable body next to me. The shallow rise and fall of Merrick's chest is the only indication of life as his battered and bruised form remains motionless.

Jax whimpers nervously at the end of the hallway, and I watch as he disappears out of sight.

What the hell happened?

"You survived. Now, if I were you, I'd get the hell out of there."

My gaze lingers on Merrick, yet surprisingly I feel nothing. No remorse, no sadness, no regret, no happiness. Just emptiness.

It's as if an abyss of nothing has swallowed my soul, and right now, I'm thankful for it.

Clatter sounds out nearby, and the click of heels echoes through the house. "Babe?"

Oh, fuck.

"Ori. Out. Now." The command spurs me into action, and I push off the ground, but my limbs feel heavy—like two noodles lifting a five pound bag of potatoes as my muscles strain to support my

weight. I manage to get myself onto my hands and knees as footsteps approach the hallway, followed by a shriek.

"God help me!" Merrick's wife fumbles around before I hear her pleading for 911 to come quickly, and I try to push to my feet, but my limbs won't bear my weight.

I'm so beyond fucked.

"There's still a way out of this."

Oh yeah? Care to fill me in on it? Cause the way I see it, I'm tres-passing and kneeling next to my half-dead professor.

"There's no such thing as 'half-dead.' There's dead or not dead. He's clearly not dead."

A strangled laugh escapes my throat.

I must be losing it. I'm having a conversation with a voice in my head, and just nearly killed someone.

The voice falls quiet and after what feels like an eternity, rhythmic footsteps echo down the hallway before two large men fill the space beside me.

I'm vaguely aware of Merrick's wife demanding they check on him first, threatening to sue them for everything they're worth if he dies. By the time they've loaded both of us into separate ambulances, I'm bordering on delirious, with a police officer climbing into the seat beside me.

My mind is a jumbled mess of broken thoughts, still grappling with the reality that Mr. Merrick attacked me while I'm cuffed to this gurney when the cop clicks his pen, holding it over a small pad of paper.

"Can you tell me what happened?"

"Sure." My words are lazy and slurred from exhaustion as I yawn deeply. "I came to walk Jax—"

"Who is Jax?"

I frown at the sudden interruption. "Mr. Harv- Merrick's dog."

The officer notes something down on a pad of paper. "Go on."

Sighing in frustration, I don't think of my wording or dial back my tone of annoyance as I walk through the events. "Well, I came to walk Jax, and I didn't need to because class was canceled, but my phone was broken, so it's not like I would have known."

"Oriana." the voice warns, and I roll my eyes.

"Oh hush, I'm trying to tell a story." The cop raises a brow but lets me continue. "Anyways, before I was so rudely interrupted, I came to walk Jax. I heard Mr. Merrick doing something that I probably shouldn't have—"

"What do you mean?"

I yawn again, my hand twitches to cover my mouth but the cuffs clatter. *Can't they just let me rest? Do I need to answer all these questions now? I'm so freaking exhausted.*

"Well, I heard someone crying when I came in, and loud banging but I didn't know what it was."

"Ori, choose your words carefully. He's not dead."

A throbbing headache radiates from my temples and I grimace. "I'm well aware that you left him alive."

The officer's brows pinch together. "Who are you talking to?"

I groan loudly. "This fucking voice. Honestly, I should have listened to him from the start and just left the house, or I should have taken Jax and not come back."

The door opens, and the cop waves someone off before noting something else down. "And what did this voice say?"

"Ori..." the voice warns again, but I promptly ignore it.

"Other than that Merrick was going to kill me?"

There's a brief pause, and the officer scribbles something down before putting his pen into his jacket. "How often do you hear this voice?"

"Ori stop fucking talking." His words are clipped, and frustration builds in me.

"You mean other than right now? He's so damn bossy."

"What's he saying?" The cop continues to note things down before pausing to look at me.

"For me to stop answering you." The realization dawns on me and my mouth snaps shut.

Oh, they probably think I have some kind of mental illness.

I'm not unconvinced that I don't, at this point.

"I tried to warn you."

You're the whole reason I'm in this mess.

The voice scoffs, and sounds incredulous as he retorts. *"Me? You're the one who refused to steal the fucking dog."*

"Alright, we're going to have to bring you to the hospital for evaluation before we get any more statements."

I nod, not trusting myself to speak anymore as he climbs out the back of the ambulance. *This is all your fault.*

"Mine?" The voice asks, as if the accusation is still just as ridiculous. *"I thought I was imaginary?"*

The door to the ambulance opens again, and a paramedic climbs in to sit beside me. As the engine roars to life, her gaze flicks to my cuffed wrists and a mix of embarrassment and fear coats my veins.

"They think I'm a monster, don't they?"

Shock flashes across her face for a moment before her expression softens. "I'm not sure what they think."

The ambulance lurches forward, and the wires attached to me sway with each movement, the gentle swish and rhythmic beeping the only sound breaking the silence for the rest of the drive.

~

It's been hours since I arrived at the hospital, and they transferred me to a private room. I'm still handcuffed to the bed like a criminal, and the voice in my head hasn't spoken since the ambulance.

Part of me is relieved by the silence, because it finally means some semblance of normalcy... but another large part of me feels more alone than ever.

I have no parents, no home, and now, the voice to blame for this mess is gone, leaving me to my torturous thoughts as I wonder what could have happened differently.

What if Rae hadn't done the spell? What if I hadn't broken my phone? What if I had just taken Jax?

The thought I keep coming back to is that, if I hadn't dropped my phone, this could've all been avoided.

A soft knock at the door interrupts my endless train of hypothetical scenarios before a doctor comes in with a police officer in tow. The silhouette of a third man in a well tailored suit and tie follows, his blonde hair neatly styled, with light grey eyes, and a pair of glasses that don't look like they help his vision at all that perch on his nose.

"Ms. Sharpe, we took the liberty of calling a public defender here to represent you. Based on our original assessment, we received a court order to detain you while you receive a mental health evaluation. Dr. Jensen is here to conduct that evaluation."

Dr. Jensen, a shorter man with dark brown hair that's been gelled back with a grey suit under his pristine white coat steps forward. He plasters on a dry smile as he pulls a stool alongside the bed. "Hello, Ms. Sharpe."

There's a pause, and I glance between all three men awkwardly. "Hi."

"Are you currently taking any medications or receiving therapy?"

I shake my head. "No, I've always been healthy. Outside of the birth control implant the nurse put down earlier, I don't take any other medications."

My heart pounds nervously. *Is this all because of what I said earlier?*

When the voice doesn't answer, my anxiety heightens.

"I see," Dr. Jensen says, nodding as he scribbles notes. "Have you experienced any recent changes, such as moving or traumatic events?"

I swallow hard. "I moved in with my best friend near the college about two months ago after my parents died."

The doctor remains impassive as he continues writing. "Have you had any trouble sleeping, eating, or concentrating since then?"

My gaze flicks to the public defender whose looking at me sympathetically. "Um, all three I guess. But that's normal, right?"

Dr. Jensen nods. "Yes, it is quite common. How do you feel you've been coping with the adjustment?"

I grit my teeth. *If they want to know whether I'm having a mental breakdown, they should just ask me.*

"I've been coping as well as I can."

"Have you used drugs or alcohol?"

"No, neither. What are you trying to ask me?"

The doctor marks a couple of things off on the paper in front of him. "Nothing at all, we're just trying to understand more about your state of mind."

"My state of mind? You want to know my state of mind?"

"Ori..." The voice warns, but I'm too caught up in my frustration to acknowledge it, let alone listen.

"My parents died in a freak car accident that never should have happened. I've been living with my best friend for months in this fucking never-ending nightmare of loneliness where no one fucking knows me. Now I'm hearing a man's voice in my head and being attacked by my professor, who was clearly hurting someone, when all I wanted to do was walk his fucking dog!"

"Ms. Sharpe, you need to calm down," the officer states flatly, but I'm not done.

"No, if you want to know how I'm doing, just imagine waking up after being attacked by a grown man, being covered in his blood, not knowing what happened, where you are, or how you're still alive.

Then, you're taken into a fucking hospital and interrogated about your mental health!" My chest heaves, and I instantly regret my outburst, but there's nothing I can do about it now.

The doctor scribbles down additional notes and checks more boxes with a sigh. "Ms. Sharpe, we're going to need to give you some medication to calm you down, and you'll be admitted to a facility for a few days to ensure you're not a danger to yourself or others. I do have one final question for you, though."

Admitted? A danger? I wouldn't hurt a fly!

"You did nearly kill—what did you call him—Mr. Harvard?"

That was you, not me!

The voice chuckles, and my gaze flicks to each of the men in the room as the doctor stands up.

"What kind of religious beliefs do you have, Ms. Sharpe?"

I frown. "Religious beliefs?"

The doctor nods, sliding his pen into his coat pocket. "Yes. Are you Christian, Catholic, Protestant, etc?"

I huff a dry laugh. "I grew up Catholic, but I don't subscribe to religion anymore."

The doctor blinks, nods once, and turns to look at both other men before leaving the room with the officer in tow. The public defender watches me with a soft expression before stepping closer. His towering form nears the bedside but stops a few feet away as my anxiety peaks.

"I'm not able to stop the court-ordered medication or treatment, but I should be able to argue to get you back home after a few days, provided that you cooperate."

My eyes widen, and I move to raise my hands as the cuffs clatter once more. "Cooperate? I didn't do anything wrong!"

His brow raises. "Records show you were found in your teacher's house, covered in his blood while he struggled to maintain basic bodily function. That's cause for concern."

I hate this guy.

The voice laughs but it sounds muffled, as if unable to help himself.

"And what happens if I don't cooperate?"

The public defender's jaw tightens. "Then you will be admitted to a psychiatric facility long-term, heavily medicated, and you'll remain there until they determine you're no longer hearing voices or a threat to society."

My heart drops, and the nurse comes back in with a vial in her hand. "Okay, Ms. Sharpe. I've got some medications to help calm you down. You may feel tired or sleepy, but it should help with your symptoms."

No. I'm not crazy, I don't need this.

"You are by their standards."

Make them stop. My internal voice is nearly pleading at this point.

"Ori, I've done enough... If I intervene any more, things will only get worse for you."

My heart races as she steps closer, pushing the needle into the vial and flipping it upside down, drawing the plunger out as she watches the lines on the side. Tears well in my eyes I glance at the public defender whose features are etched with tense concern as he watches her.

"I'm here with you," the voice says softly. *"You'll be okay."*

Panic wells up within me as she straps a band around my bicep. She leans forward to insert a syringe into my arm, leaving the cannula in before giving me an apologetic look. "This may give you a cold sensation at first... but you'll be asleep soon."

I glance between her and the public defender with wide eyes. My other arm twitches with the urge to escape as my handcuff clatters slightly.

This can't be happening to me.

"It's okay, Ori. I'm here. Just relax."

His voice is so soft, reassuring even, and though part of me blames the voice for everything, there's something comforting about him, whether it's a figment of my imagination or not.

She injects the cold fluid into my vein, and my arm starts to tingle and burn as my hand flexes against the sensation. My heart races, quickly pushing the liquid through my veins as she cleans the remnants of packaging, throwing away the syringe and her gloves.

My heart rate slows, and my mind starts to grow foggy as my gaze lands on the public defender who watches the nurse as she moves around the room busily.

Even though there's people in the room with me, I can't help but feel more alone than ever.

"You're not alone, Ori."

Easy to say that when you're not cuffed to a bed surrounded by strangers.

My arms start to feel heavy, and a stray tear rolls down my cheek.

At least tell me your name.

There's a moment of silence before the voice answers. *"You can call me Seir."*

My eyelids get heavier as I blink slowly, locking eyes with the public defender as his jaw tightens.

Will you be here when I wake up?

There's a brief pause, and my blinks last longer as each one comes slower than the last.

"I hope so."

Chapter 5

Time is nothing more than a blur.

It's an odd feeling to not only lose track of, but not know the concept of time, with large gaps in memory, and a heavy fog over my mind making it impossible to comprehend the world around me.

My limbs feel heavy, like they haven't moved in days as I stir on the bed with a mess of chaotic thoughts.

What day is it? Where am I? Is this a dream?

The quiet of the room is maddening, and a foul smell makes my stomach churn.

I'm gonna—

I turn over to see a bucket beside the bed, and I pull it closer before hurling bile into it. My nose scrunches at the rancid acidic smell, and the half-full bucket tells me this isn't the first time I've woken up this way.

Using the back of my hand to wipe my mouth, I push the bowl away onto the side table and sit up unsteadily, glancing around my familiar townhouse bedroom. Light pours in from the window, and birds sing cheerfully, entirely oblivious to the dreary feeling hanging in the air around me.

At least I'm home.

Vague memories of the hospital are broken up in my mind. I remember bits and pieces of people coming in to question me, but they were always interrupted or sent away by the public defender.

In fact, come to think of it, I can't remember a moment where he wasn't there in any of those fragmented memories. He'd sit in the corner of the room, with his laptop on the table as he worked. Though I don't know if he was there just while I was lucid enough to see him or if he'd left periodically. All my memories are so disjointed that it's hard to know for certain.

My heart pounds as I consider the events leading up to this moment.

....Seir...?

The answering silence is deafening.

Did I really have a psychotic break? Was it all a figment of my imagination?

My head whirls with questions, but footsteps down the hall grow closer, and a soft knock echoes into the room.

"Ori?" Rae's voice is like music to my ears, and my shoulders sag in relief.

"Come in," I manage to croak out as the door hinges squeak. Rae takes a tentative step inside, closing the door behind her with a bottle of water in her hand. She scrunches her nose and places the water bottle against my knee before stepping further away to the door, looking at me apologetically.

"Sorry, it just stinks in here."

Tears well up in my eyes as I nod. "I need to shower, and the smell of my vomit is going to make me vomit more if I don't get rid of this bucket."

She laughs, stepping over to the window to open it before pausing. "Are you okay?"

I suck in a deep breath of blissfully fresh air. "I'm not, but, I think I will be."

She moves to the window and leans against the wall. "Do you wanna talk about what happened?"

I purse my lips, chewing the inside of my cheek nervously. Rae's been my best friend for years, and we've shared everything together. There's no way I can't tell her this.

"After that night, when the power went out..." Her gaze flicks to mine, "I heard a voice..."

She blinks before excitement paints her features, and she leans forward, "What kind of voice?"

Don't get too excited, Rae. He was just make-believe.

I wring my hands together and cross my legs on the bed, "It was some guy's voice. At first he just was sassy and laughed at my internal dialogue, and it scared the shit out of me, but I thought it was just temporary. But then he was still there when I woke up in the morning, so I panicked and broke my phone. When I went to walk Jax, he was warning me to leave..."

She frowns, and the tense look on her face tells me that she's more concerned about this part of the story than me hearing a voice.

"What happened at Mr. Merricks, Ori?"

I swallow hard and chew my cheek more. "When I got there, I heard him say something but it was muffled through the wall. It wasn't until I heard banging and crying that I realized something was wrong. I tried to pretend I had just gotten there, but..." She stays silent as I take a ragged breath. "The voice said Merrick knew and that I should just take the dog for a walk and not come back. I should have listened to him." Tears trail down my cheeks before falling to the bed. "When I got back he was waiting and chased me, saying I knew too much. He attacked me, and I was about to pass out when the voice told me to let him in..."

Looking at her hesitantly, there's no judgement or sympathy on her face, only anger and understanding. "I was desperate, Rae, so I agreed. The next thing I know, I'm waking up covered in Merrick's blood and he's almost dead beside me."

To her credit, she doesn't balk or seem surprised. "Have you heard the voice since?"

I shake my head. "Not since they medicated me. I don't even know how long that stuff lasts."

She winces. "They said it was a long working medication that lasts around twenty four hours after you take it, and stays in your system for up to five days..."

"When was my last dose?"

"Roughly four hours ago... You throw up every time you take it for the next few hours. This is the first time you've actually been up after taking it though."

I feel the blood drain from my face. "How long have I been out?"

She fidgets nervously before wrapping her arms around her body. "You've been home for four days. They had you admitted for three."

Four days. It's been an entire week.

"Don't freak out... You look like you're going to freak out, Ori."

I blink at her, my voice barely a whisper. "I just wish my life was normal."

She grimaces before looking at me with a raised brow. "Yeah, well, so much for that. Do you think you're okay to go to classes today?"

Weighing the exhaustion in my body, I nod. "Yeah. I need.. normalcy."

"Okay, I'll let the school know. They asked for me to escort you between classes just in case—"

"Just in case what? Just in case I go ape-shit and tear apart another student?"

Rae puts her hands up defensively. "Listen, I know this is a lot, but we're going to have to play their game. We're lucky they even allowed you to stay. Merrick's wife has gone scorched earth to get you expelled based on religious principle."

I roll my eyes. "I'm not religious, so she can suck a dick."

For a moment, I almost think I hear a soft chuckle, but it's so soft, I almost miss it.

"Well, you might not be, but DCC and Merrick are. She's trying to say it was a hate crime."

I groan loudly. "You have to be joking."

Rae shakes her head. "Nope. Anyway, let's worry about all that another day. Get cleaned up, and take care of that," she points to the bucket beside the bed with a scrunched face, "before we get breakfast."

I yawn deeply as she opens the door, pausing halfway through. "Oh and Ori, thanks for trusting me enough to tell me what happened."

My heart clenches, and I nod. "Sisters."

She grins at me, and the tightness in my chest grows. "Sisters."

I watch her disappear through the doorway and heave a sigh.

So, are you there and just ignoring me?

"It seemed like an inappropriate time to interrupt."

Would have been nice to know you were there when I woke up.

I know that part of me is rationalizing that him still being here is an indication that the medication isn't working, which either means it's not strong enough or I'm not actually crazy.

I really hope it's the latter.

There's a long pause, and I start to silently scold myself for being so upfront when he responds.

"I had to take care of something. It didn't appear clear when you were going to wake up."

I frown as his choice of words.

You had to take care of something?

"Even after everything that has happened, and being on medication that should, for all intents and purposes, stop you from hearing voices, you still think I'm just a figment of your imagination, don't you?"

My stomach turns uncomfortably as my gaze slides to the bowl beside the bed. If I don't get rid of it soon, I'll end up in a vicious cycle of dry heaving.

I'm going to get out of bed before I vomit more, but I want answers, Seir.

The resulting deep chuckle in response flips my stomach for reasons I can't explain, and I push to my feet unsteadily, holding my breath as I weakly carry the bucket to the bathroom.

Dumping the contents and flushing, I look in the mirror to see my sunken in cheeks, the dark circles under my eyes and the paleness of my skin.

I look like shit.

"You look like you've been through hell."

I laugh quietly, because he's not wrong.

Maybe just less fire and brimstone.

He laughs, and I find myself caught between scared of whatever this is that's happening to me but equally wanting to know more about... well, everything. There's no way this isn't real, not when I'm on medication, and he seems so incredibly real in how he talks.

This means I'm not crazy right?

"You are not. Although, to them, you might seem to be."

*So, I **am** crazy?*

"Did I say that?"

No. I just...

"Just what, Oriana?"

My heart stutters, and I tug my t-shirt overhead, tossing it to the floor before letting my pajamas fall to the ground. I wrap my arms around my body.

How do I know you're more than just a voice in my head?

"Look in the mirror."

My heart pounds, and I glance up to see a lock of my hair glide from in front of my shoulder to behind it, with the ghost of a touch grazing my cheek as a shiver wracks through my body.

Oh.

Seir laughs quietly, and I frown.

Wait so why didn't you just do that before, why did you say you needed me to let you in.

There's a long moment of silence, and I twist the knob to the shower before waiting for it to warm up. It's not until I'm climbing into the steady stream of water that he finally answers.

"I may have been able to hear you, hear your surroundings, and see what you could see, but I couldn't actually do anything. You had to let me in before I was able to physically stop him."

I raise my brow, reaching for the shampoo.

You did more than just stop him.

"He deserved worse."

The memory of Merrick's body in a heap beside my flickers into my mind.

What made you decide against killing him?

There's another long moment of silence as I massage the shampoo into my hair before grasping the body wash and lathering it over my skin. I'm nearly done rinsing the suds from my body when he finally responds.

"The only reason he still breathes is because I knew the repercussions for you if I ended his life. So I brought him as close to the end as I dared to."

My pulse quickens, and I'm not imagining the way the shower curtain waves suddenly.

Why even help me at all?

The silence stretches between us, and I mindlessly finish washing off. By the time I've turned off the faucet, and climbed out of the shower, I still haven't gotten an answer. In fact, the only response I receive is silence until I'm wrapped in a towel, and stepping out of the bathroom.

Okay, maybe that question was out of bounds.

"What question?"

I frown, and a mixture of embarrassment and frustration coats my veins.

Nothing. Don't worry about it.

"Alright."

Walking to the bedroom, I pull on a pleated skirt and blouse before grabbing my backpack and hoisting it over my shoulder.

"Ori, lets go!" Rae's voice calls from the other side of the house, and I hurry down the hallway. My body still feels exhausted and foggy from the medication as I turn the corner, seeing her petite form standing near the front door.

"About time," she grins, and gives me a once-over. "How are you feeling?"

"Exhausted, but ready to not be in bed and laying down."

She laughs, her smile reaching her eyes as she hooks her arm through mine. "Who are you, and what have you done with the Ori I've known for the past two months that only wanted to binge-watch Supernatural and fall down YouTube rabbit holes?"

A choked laugh crawls out my throat, and both of us look at one another in surprise before laughing in earnest.

"I guess the medication is working then?"

"Don't tell her."

Guilt tears through me within milliseconds as I nod. "Yeah, I'm feeling okay."

She keeps her arm hooked in mine as she glances down the road. "Good. I'm glad to have my sister back."

I've never lied to her before.

"You are not doing it maliciously. It's for her safety as much as yours."

The thought that we could both be in danger is sobering, and I swallow hard against the lump in my throat.

"An email came through this morning, they finally found a sub for Religious Studies while Mr. Merrick is recovering. Are you going to swap classes when he comes back?"

"I don't think I can change it, especially not this late."

"Well, hopefully the investigation into whatever happened results in his permanent removal. Apparently your public defender has quite the history of winning cases, and he got some hotshot investigative team involved, so they're looking into why Merrick attacked you in the first place."

My eyes widen and snap to her. "Have they found anything?"

Did you know about this?

Rae shakes her head. "Nothing yet that I know of."

"I'm aware of it, yes."

I don't have the heart to ask if he knows anything else, and my focus is pulled front and center as Rae squeezes my arm. "Are you okay?"

I blink at her, seeing the concerned look etched across her features. "Uh, yeah, why?"

"Well, you got this kinda dazed look on your face for a second there."

"Oh, it must be the meds. They're making me kinda out of it."

"Okay, well, I've got ya. Don't worry about focusing until we get to school. Are you going to be okay during class though?"

I swallow. Lying to her just doesn't sit well with me, but Seir's words ring in my ears as I nod. "Yeah I'll have to make it work. I can't afford to fail."

We spend the rest of the short walk to campus in relative silence, minus rhetorical comments here and there from Rae as we near the front doors. Eyes follow us as we walk through the main hallway, and my heart races as people whisper when we pass by.

I guess word spread about what happened.

"Ignore them. They're irrelevant."

A guy up ahead makes a remark to his friend, and they all laugh as they look at me. My cheeks warm, and I glance forward, avoiding eye contact as we head to our lockers.

Another random student I've never spoken to leans over with a smug grin. "Heard you lost your marbles, Ori." He high-fives his friend before they laugh, turning in the other direction.

Rae huffs in annoyance, giving the group the middle finger as they walk away. "Just ignore them, Ori. They're all dumb."

A sudden clatter and rolling sounds echo through the hall as a bunch of marbles go sprawling in every direction, and a handful of students break out in laughter.

Right. Ignore them.

The main culprit, Danny, tucks the now empty bag into his pocket with a vicious smile and I grind my molars. He made my life a living hell long before this all happened, even going so far as to make dead parent jokes mere days after they died.

I can only imagine how insufferable he'll be now.

Danny turns to face his friend when he suddenly teeters to the side, screaming in pain as he hobbles onto one leg. He lifts his pant leg to where his ankle has swollen, and he limps to keep his weight off it.

Holy shit.

The answering barely restrained laugh has blood draining from my face.

Did you just do that?

Humor drips from Seir's voice as he answers. *"I might have expedited the tear in his Achilles. The guy should really be more careful. Sports can be a blessing and a curse."*

I can't fight the ghost of a smile that tugs at my lips.

"Turd is getting what he deserves." My eyes widen as I look at Rae, who just shrugs innocently in response. "Come on. We should get going if we're going to be on time."

The rest of the walk to class isn't any quieter, but after seeing Danny's immediate karma, I find it easier to ignore the whispers and comments being tossed around.

By the time we make it to Religious Studies, things feel mostly normal. Pushing past a group of students, we walk into the room, and the hairs on the back of my neck stand on end. My gaze slides along the rows of seats from the back of the class to the front, where a tall, dark-haired man in a black, expensive looking, well-tailored suit stands with his back facing the students, placing a stack of books onto the desk.

Goosebumps break out over my skin as Rae leads me away from the doorway, and I finally tear my eyes from the man at the front as she guides us to our seats. I ease into my chair, but when my face tilts up one more, my eyes gravitate to whom I assume is the new substitute professor.

My heart may very well beat out of my chest as he turns to face the class, and piercing ocean blue eyes scan the room. I swallow as he drags his hand through his dark hair, before leaning back onto his desk. The muscles in his forearms flex, his knuckles turn white as he braces himself against the wooden edge, and his suit tapers down his muscular form with bare skin peering out from between the open buttons at the top of his dress shirt.

Holy fuck he's beautiful.

His lips twitch with restrained humor when he looks directly at me.

"Pleasure to finally meet you, Oriana."

Chapter 6

Wait...

The smile on his face turns earnest as he fails to suppress a small laugh, and I stare at him in disbelief.

You're my...

His eyes pin me in place as my heart leaps into my throat. There's no way this is real life right now that he's my substitute professor.

"For the foreseeable future, yes."

My entire body warms as the realization hits me.

Oh. Oh, and you heard me say that...

He laughs under his breath at his desk, but I can hear it loud and clear in my mind. His answering smile flashing in my direction tells me all I need to know as I groan internally, pressing my forehead to my desk.

"It's alright, your secrets are safe with me."

I tilt my head up, only to see his gaze still fixated on me with barely restrained humor painted across his features.

I'm still acclimating to the fact that you have a body.

*"A **beautiful** body."*

The teasing in his voice is clear, and my entire body flushes. The chatter around us quiets as the last students take their seats, and I lean back, watching as his attention sweeps over the room.

"I'm not certain where your professor left off with your studies, but we will be covering some basics before diving into demonology over the course of the next few weeks."

Hearing his voice in person is an experience in itself. It's just as it was when it resonated inside my mind, but hearing it like this...

It means it was all real.

This really wasn't a figment of my imagination.

Seir rolls up his sleeves another inch, and I track the movement before dragging my eyes to his once more. Another wave of heat washes over me when he's already looking in my direction.

A student in the front row raises his hand, and Seir's gaze flicks to him, "Speak."

The command sends a shiver through my body, and the student stammers, lowering his hand, "I—uh, sir. We were studying varying rituals that occur in each religion before Mr. Merrick went on leave. We stopped at the soul binding and soul claiming rituals."

A few heads turn in my direction at the mention of his name, and I fight the urge to squirm as I reach into my bag for water, pretending to not hear the topic.

"Great. That's not what we're covering now. Any further concerns?"

The student shakes his head nervously, and Seir flashes him a disarming smile when another student raises their hand timidly. "Sorry, what was your name?"

Seir's eyes flick to mine as I take a sip from my water bottle. "The name is Mr. Harvard."

Liquid gets caught in my throat, and I sputter, coughing as water goes down the wrong hole.

Oh my god.

His lips twitch as the student lowers his hand, and another in the front row raises theirs. "Do you know when Mr. Merrick will be back?"

My heart thumps loudly as Seir tilts his head. "No. As of right now, Merrick is on medical leave with no set return date."

Chatter erupts among the students, and Seir raises his hands to silence them. "Any speculation on why will result in your permanent removal from this class. Understood?"

Our eyes meet again, and agreement murmurs from all corners of the room.

Thank you.

"Do you remember what I said about them?"

I frown, resisting the urge to shake my head in response.

"They're irrelevant, Oriana."

So why are you here, then?

He gives me a look, like I should know the answer to that before stepping to his desk to grab a small stack of books, and handing them out to each row.

"Before we dive further into theology, I'm going to start with basics. Can anyone tell me what a demon is?"

A girl in the front row raises her hand shyly, and Seir points to her. "Speak."

Her hand drops into her lap. "They're evil beings."

Seir's clicks his tongue, and he tilts his head. "They're all completely evil?"

She nods. "Yes, Mr. Harvard."

Oh my God.

A sudden laugh escapes me, and I cough to cover it as heads turn my way.

"Anything you'd like to add, Ms. Sharpe?"

I blink at him.

Are you seriously asking me to weigh in? Ninety percent of these people will hate my answer.

"What are you afraid of?"

The challenge in his gaze is clear, and I clear my throat as Rae gives my desk a light kick.

"Demons in most cultures are just spirits who commit acts that are seen as evil. They're claimed by most religions to be the main culprit to tempt humans to do evil or malicious acts. In Christianity, most, if not all demons are viewed as fallen angels who might still maintain their angelic traits even though they have been cast out of Heaven after a rebellion against God, and they are loyal to or often described as aligning with Lucifer."

There's a long moment of silence as Seir stares at me before turning his attention to the rest of the class. "Very good, Ms. Sharpe. That is all theologically accurate. Does anyone have anything else to add?"

When no one else speaks up, Seir picks up a book from the desk, facing the cover toward us.

"I'd like for you all to spend the rest of the hour reading the first section of this book. It will help you understand more about demons from various cultural perspectives."

Whispering erupts among the students as the sound of pages turning echoes through the room.

Rae leans closer. "Ori," she whispers, "What the hell?"

I reluctantly tear my gaze from Seir to glance over at her. "What?"

"What do you mean, 'What?' Do you know this guy?"

She gestures to Seir at the front, who is flipping through a textbook, pretending not to listen.

"Would you rather I stare directly at both of you while I eavesdrop? Besides, even without your perspective, her whispers are not exactly subtle."

My heart skips a beat, and I notice several students glancing our way. "No, I don't know him."

Have I ever said how much I despise lying to her?

"Once or twice."

Rae frowns, casting another doubtful look at Seir before settling back in her chair. I can tell she's not fully convinced and would bet she'll ask me again later today or tonight.

Are you worried she's going to tell someone?

There's a long pause, and I see Seir's gaze flick to her before landing on me.

"You trust her?"

With my life.

My answer is immediate, and without hesitation. Seir's answering flash of surprise quickly disappears before he scans the room again.

"That kind of loyalty is rare. I hope it is not misplaced."

I don't bother asking for permission; it's likely the closest answer to a yes I'll get. Considering that it's mostly my life that I'm wagering, I understand why Seir would want me to be overly cautious.

But Rae would never betray me, lie or tell someone something that would hurt me.

No. She would sooner lie to someone to keep me safe and out of a hospital, even if I joke that she'd do the opposite.

Glancing over to Seir at his desk, his ocean-blue eyes find mine again, and for a brief moment, everything else in the room fades away. It's like his gaze sucks me in, and I'm being held captive by the sea.

Seir, do you know why this happened?

I know it's tied with whatever spell Rae did that night, but I need confirmation that he's just as confused as I am.

His lips purse thoughtfully.

"I've been summoned before, occasionally, but never like this. So I'm not sure how to answer your question, Ori."

I frown at his choice of words, and I'm too nervous to ask him directly who or what he is. But still...

That's a better answer than I expected.

His lips twitch, and he returns to the textbook in front of him.

The rest of class is uneventful.

I spend the remainder of the hour reading the introduction to demonology, which mostly reiterates what I already knew. The text however does mention that in some philosophies, demons are seen as divine inspiration rather than inherently evil—they're considered more of a form of divine power and spirit.

Three minutes before the hour ends, students begin packing up, and a few move to the front to speak with Seir. As he converses with them, Rae jabs my shoulder roughly. "Ori, why are you staring at him?"

My cheeks flush, and a restrained huff of laughter resonates in my mind as Seir's gaze flicks to me before returning to the person in front of him.

"I don't know what you're talking about."

Rae scoffs. "Stop lying! I know you're lying to me, and you're terrible at it."

Fuck.

My heart thrashes, and I glance around. "Not here. I'll explain, but not right now."

She blinks, seeming to get the hint for privacy before she nods. "Okay, later."

I stand up, packing my things into my bags when my pen drops to the ground, rolling a couple feet away, and I crouch down to grab it. When I straighten and turn around, Liam—the guy I've had a crush on since middle school—holds out the demonology book toward me.

Taking it from his grasp, my mind is a jumbled mess as I step closer to my desk. "Thanks, Liam."

His answering smile seems genuine as he hoists his bag over his shoulder. "Anytime. Oriana, right?"

I nod. "Just Ori is fine."

Rae stands just behind him, her eyes wide as she subtly gestures that she's about to leave to avoid interrupting us.

"Ah, Ori. That was cool that you knew that much about demons, earlier. Did you study it in another class?"

I resist the urge to make a sarcastic remark about being raised by devil-fearing parents and simply shake my head. "No, just, passionate about learning, I guess."

He smiles. "Ah, well, do you mind if I walk you to your next class? We have English together, right?"

My heart flutters, and every emotion or desire I'd had about Liam resurfaces as I nod. "Sure. I'd like that."

Liam leads the way out the door, and I feel Seir's burning gaze in the back of my head as we walk to our next class.

Chapter 7

"So, how have you been?"

The question somehow takes me off guard, and although I instinctively open my mouth to answer, it snaps shut. He's asking as if we're old friends, and that couldn't be further from the truth.

"Uh, I've been better, but I'm okay now."

He grimaces. "I didn't mean to be inconsiderate. I meant about losing your parents. Forgot about all the rumors going around. Sorry."

I spot Rae glancing over her shoulder as she walks ahead of us, and my cheeks flush. "Oh, you're fine. It was a lot to lose them... But time heals everything, right?"

I laugh awkwardly, and he nods as if it's the most sensible thing he's heard all year.

"Yeah, yeah. My dad always says that God puts challenges in our path to strengthen us."

I blink, and his lips thin into a forced smile.

"This is incredibly painful to watch."

My cheeks burn for a whole different reason.

No one said you were invited.

"You're quite literally broadcasting this to me."

Uh. How do I stop?

There's a brief pause as we turn the final corner toward our next class. I'm almost resigned to the fact that he doesn't have a solution when he answers, albeit, reluctantly.

"Imagine you're covering your mind with something. A towel, blanket, cloth. See if that works for you."

My brows pull together, and I imagine pulling something akin to a mental blanket over my mind.

Seir is a silly goose, and he smells like stinky feet.

There's no response, and a sense of satisfaction rifles through me as we turn the final corner to class. When I spot Rae near the door, she gives me a small wave before hurrying to her own class down the hall.

"Say, there's a study group I'm in, they're having a bit of a party this Friday to blow off some steam. Do you wanna come?"

I watch as he sets his bag down next to my usual desk. "Uh, sure."

He's going to sit next to me? Is this the twilight zone?

His smile widens. "Great. I can borrow my dad's car and pick you up at six-thirty. Text me your address?" He holds his phone. "I guess we need to exchange numbers first, though."

Something akin to nervousness rushes through me, and I nod, taking his phone from him to put Rae's number in.

"Right. My phone is broken though, so I put Rae's number in since we live together."

"Oh, alright. Cool."

I slide into my seat, and a tentative, giddy excitement washes over me.

Friday at six-thirty, it is.

The hour feels like an eternity as the professor drags on, but Liam doesn't say anything else to me. Even as class ends, and a handful of other students within his normal social circle turn to talk to him, he leaves me out of it.

I can't decide if I'm annoyed or relieved that I don't have to pretend to like them. Most of his friends have always seemed fake or disingenuous.

Unfortunately, that leaves me no choice but to be disingenuous back or fully avoid them.

I've been particularly fine with the latter.

By the time I leave class, Rae is already waiting for me. "Can you tell me what the hell is going on?" she whispers loudly, and I glance around.

"Not yet. After school."

"Why was Liam talking to you? Did he want something?"

I shake my head. "He wants me to come to some party on Friday."

She rears back with her eyes as wide as saucers. "Not that you shouldn't have been invited, but isn't that a little out of the blue?"

I know it is, but part of me hopes it's genuine. Actually, the entirety of me wants it to be real. I'd spent years daydreaming about hanging out with Liam—being asked out, going to movies, running into him at the mall with my mom.

None of it ever happened, but the schoolgirl crush in me is ecstatic, and I can't shake it.

"Okay, and what's with Mr. Harvard?"

My eyes widen as I glance at her.

She knows Mr. Harvard was my nickname for Merrick, so there's no way in hell she doesn't know something is going on.

I sigh deeply. "I'll explain when we get home."

Her gaze lingers on me for a moment before she turns back to the hallway in front of us, and it's all I can do not to overthink about what her reaction will be.

The next two classes pass by without incident, other than the occasional remark about me losing my mind or someone's concern about being attacked.

In fact, it's so quiet that I almost miss Seir's random commentary and cheerful retorts.

Okay, more than almost.

It feels oddly lonely without his random interjections, and I'm about to lift whatever cover I had put over my mind when Rae holds the front door open for me, and hooks her arm through mine as we get further from campus.

"So, are you going to 'fess up?"

I glance around, and we're far enough away from everyone that they won't be able to eavesdrop, so I decide to let her in. "Remember the voice?"

She squeezes my arm reassuringly. "Yeah."

Here goes nothing.

"It's him."

I look at her to gauge her reaction, and her brows furrow in confusion. "What do you mean?"

My palms grow sweaty, and my heart races.

What if she doesn't believe me? Oh god, what if I'm making a mistake?

But I've already come this far, so I stubbornly double down. "I mean, it's him. He's the voice, but in person."

Rae lets out an awkward laugh. "So you're telling me the voice you heard in your head is the same as his voice?"

Embarrassment washes over me, and I stop walking, glancing around before giving her a deadpan look.

"I mean, even though I was on medication, I could still hear his voice. And then when we walked into class, he said it was nice to finally meet me in person before introducing himself as Mr. Harvard."

Her eyes widen, and she blows out a breath. "Holy shit."

I let out a relieved sigh, and we continue walking in silence, giving her time to process the information.

The silence is maddening though, and I find myself itching to lift the cover and reach out to him. It's as if our interactions are a hit of a drug, making me feel something after not feeling anything for months.

In fact, I've strangely felt more myself this past week—minus being admitted and medicated—than I have since my parents died.

I flip the cover off my mind, and anxiety rises.

Seir?

The silence that follows only deepens my doubts, even though what happened in the classroom was undeniably real.

What if this is all in my head? What if I made up everything in the classroom?

The rest of the walk is a blur as my mind races to confront reality. It's not until we're walking through the door of the apartment that I notice the change in Rae's demeanor.

"Hey, are you okay?"

Rae looks up after pulling her shoes off. "Yeah I'm good. I guess that was just a lot to take in, but it makes sense now why he called himself Mr. Harvard to everyone."

I shake my head. "After everything that has happened, I wouldn't blame you for thinking I'm insane."

She just laughs, tossing a wink in my direction. "You're definitely insane, but not in the way you think."

I push my shoes aside and sigh as she heads toward the kitchen. "Want anything for dinner?"

My stomach grumbles, but I shake my head. "I'm okay. I'm actually going to lie down for a bit. Today took it out of me."

Her eyes linger on me, the concern on her face evident as she nods slightly. "Okay. Just let me know if you need anything."

With each step down the hallway, my legs slowly grow more heavy as I push past the bedroom door. My gaze scans the area, and a mixture of apprehension and comfort washes over me.

This room is kind of where it all started.

My bag hits the floor with a thud, and I collapse onto the bed.

Maybe tomorrow I'll wake up and all of this will have been a dream.

Chapter 8

The rest of the week passes in relative silence.

Wednesday and Thursday go by with little to no word from Seir. I've felt more normal than ever without taking the anti-psychotic medication, and surprisingly, Liam has continued to walk me to class.

The only confusing part has been Seir. On Thursday, he was distant, completely in teacher mode as he continued to walk us through the basics of various cultures religions. If it wasn't for the random comment in my mind here or there, I'd be wondering if I had imagined everything.

Part of me wondered if I'd said or done something to upset him because of how frequently my questions or statements went ignored, but the other part of me just figured he was busy, and it's not like he chose to be tied to my mind.

Or maybe he's just giving me space to feel like myself again after everything that happened.

It's not until Friday after my last class that I hear from him as I change out of my blouse and pleated skirt into a flowy, thigh-high sundress.

"What's the occasion?"

I freeze, dropping my brush to the ground with a clatter.

Oh, so now he wants to talk?

You're talking now?

"Well my mouth isn't moving, but yes. Is that a problem?"

Outside of you ignoring me all day?

"I wasn't ignoring you."

Not answering me is ignoring, unless you have another word for it.

A chuckle echoes into my mind, and I frown.

If you don't want to talk through whatever connection this is, it's fine. We don't have to. I don't want you to feel like you have to respond.

"You're overthinking my intentions, Ori. I was busy with some sensitive issues, so I closed off. It must have stopped you from coming through as much as it stopped me from projecting."

I guess it's sound reasoning, he does have his own life to live.

"So, what's the occasion?"

I glance in the mirror at my dress, adjusting the spaghetti straps and smoothing the black material down my body.

Someone invited me to a party tonight.

There's a long moment of silence, and my stomach flips.

"Is Rae going?"

No, she's not part of the friend group. Why?

"So, it's just you?"

Yes. What's the issue?

"I don't like the thought of you going by yourself."

I raise a brow and an awkward laugh escapes me.

You're joking.

"Does it sound like I'm joking?"

You're not my dad.

His voice is tight as he responds.

"Doesn't change the fact that I don't want you going alone."

"Ori, he's here!"

I'm leaving to go to the party. Are we going to have a problem, Seir?

The response is silence. Unsure if he's shut himself off, I grab my purse and head to the front door.

Rae notices my expression and blinks. "What's wrong?"

"Men."

She bursts out laughing, and I give her an exasperated look. "Enough said. Here," she hands me her old flip phone, "In case of emergencies. It's got a shit battery but, it will dial 911 if needed."

I swallow, giving her a tight hug before stepping out the door.

My nerves are frayed with each step toward the car parked on the side of the road. The engine rumbles to life, and I see Liam's blonde mess of hair behind the wheel as he unlocks the door with a click.

"Doesn't even get the door, what a gentleman."

I don't miss the sarcasm in Seir's voice and I suppress an eye roll. *You think you'd do better?*

A genuine laugh sounds out, and I pull open the car door.

"I'm not even going to answer that one. I think we both know."

My cheeks flush.

It's not like this is a date. It's just him picking me up to go to a party.

He goes silent as I slide into the passenger seat.

Liam shoots a grin in my direction. "Hey, Ori."

"Hi." I cringe awkwardly at my own response. "Thanks for the ride."

"Yeah, anytime. The gangs already there. They were playing beer pong before I left."

"Ah, I've never played that before."

We pull up to a red light, and relief washes over me now that the car isn't in motion, but he turns to look at me with wide eyes. "You've never played beer pong?"

I shake my head. "No, or any other drinking games for that matter. I went right into college after highschool, and didn't long for drinking much."

The light turns green, and a car honks behind us as he accelerates, sending my heart lurching into my throat. "Okay, well, we're fixing that tonight."

We finally pull up to a large house with a handful of cars parked in the driveway and loud music blaring from inside.

Nervous excitement brims inside of me, and I feel a chaotic rumble in my limbs. It's like part of me looks forward to experiencing this, whatever tonight might bring.

Liam parks, turning off the ignition and leans back. "Just stick close to me if you decide to drink at all, okay? The guys here are chill, but," his gaze lingers on my mouth, "I'd rather you stay near me."

Not trusting my voice with my heart thrashing wildly, I just nod in response, and we head inside. The bass reverberates through my chest as we make our way through the front door, passing by a crowd of unfamiliar faces until we descend the stairs.

Chatter and laughter sound out and cheers erupt once Liam is halfway down the steps.

"There he is!" A man no older than Liam bellows, walking over with two beers and offering one to Liam.

"And who is this?" another guy asks, peering around Liam to look at me, his eyes scanning me up and down.

Liam places his hand low on the small of my back. "This is Ori. We go to school together."

A girl in a short red dress walks over and runs her fingers through the length my hair. "Ori, is that short for something?"

"Um, Oriana."

She beams. "Aw, that's such a cute name! Do you want a drink?" She hooks her arm into mine and leads me to a table away from the guys.

"Uh, sure."

"I'm Lisa," she says, glancing over me. "You look like you need to loosen up. Let's do shots."

"Shots!" someone yells behind me, and everyone cheers.

This has to be a frat party or something.

Lisa pours a bunch of shots and mixes me a drink before handing both over. "Okay, Oriana, let's see what you're made of!"

"Don't let us down, Ori!" someone shouts, and my chest swells with exhilaration.

Lisa and I throw back our shots, and it takes all my willpower to swallow the burning liquid.

I gag as a shiver runs down my spine. "What the hell was that?"

"Here," Lisa says, lifting her straw to my mouth. "Chase it with this."

I take a sip, and the liquid burns my throat, leaving a terrible after-taste as I cough. "That was just as bad."

Lisa giggles, taking a sip from the straw with a shrug. "You get used to it."

After another two shots, my body feels warm, and I'm watching Liam and another guy play beer pong when Lisa approaches with another shot glass.

"Lets do body shots." She has a sly look on her face, and it sends a surge of heat through my body that isn't from the alcohol.

"Oriana." Seir's voice is warning, but I promptly ignore it.

He's been distant all week, and now he thinks he knows what's best for me?

That's a crock of shit.

"Let's do it."

Her face lights up. "Liam! Henry! Body shots!"

Cheers erupt as she turns to me, handing me the shot. "Be careful not to spill." She pulls the seam of my cleavage aside, guiding me to tuck the shot between my breasts and the material of my dress, before putting one in her own cleavage.

She hands a pack of salt to Liam and Henry before moving to stand beside me. Liam moves in close, his eyes glazed slightly as he glances down to the shot.

"Shot, shot, shot!" The crowd chants, and it sends a nervous excitement through my veins.

Liam tears the salt pack and leans in, his free hand cupping the other side of my neck as he licks the soft skin between my neck and shoulder.

My breath catches in my lungs at how close he is, and I'm completely frozen.

Liam, oblivious to my internal struggles, pours the salt over the wet patch of skin as rogue crystals trail into my dress and onto the floor.

Henry and Lisa finish their body shot beside us as cheers erupt, and Liam gets a look on his face that makes my stomach churn uncomfortably. He leans in and his tongue glides across the salt on my skin before he bends down to my cleavage to wrap his lips around the shot glass.

He bends low, far lower than necessary as his fingers dig into my biceps painfully. It's over in a second as he tilts his head back to take the shot before pulling the glass away with a triumphant grin, and one of the guys hands him a lime.

"Shots!" Lisa sings out, handing me a glass from the table and I throw it back without hesitation. The liquid burns, but the sensation is muted as I take a sip of my drink.

I'm not even sure why I avoided drinking before this. This is great.

My head spins slightly, and I cradle the drink against my chest.

"Ori, did you even eat today?"

Nope.

"Fuck—"

I can't help but giggle, and Lisa taps on Liam's arm. "I think she needs some fresh air."

Liam turns toward me, swaying slightly. "Let's go out back for a minute."

He wraps his hand around mine and tugs me up the stairs behind him as the world spins even more.

Is this what being drunk is like?

"Yes."

I fight the urge to giggle at his clipped responses.

I like it.

"You like it for now. You're going to hate it tomorrow."

You say funny things, beautiful man.

Abrupt laughter sounds out from the other end of the connection and I can't help but smile.

Liam leads me between crowds of people to the backyard, where people are half-naked, making out with music blaring. He hesitates, glancing at me before tugging me back inside and up the stairs.

"Where are we going?" I ask loudly over the music, but he doesn't hear me and keeps pulling me in along behind him.

The music is quieter on the second floor, and he opens a door, leading me inside as he shuts the door behind us, throwing the room into darkness.

It's a bedroom.

Seir's voice is a low growl that sends a jolt of fear through me. *"Ori—"*

I know.

My stomach churns uncomfortably as he opens the window, pulling the curtains apart to let in a breeze. He sits down on the edge of the bed and pats the space beside him and the wall.

The room spins as I take another step and I nearly stumble, but Liam shoots to his feet, catching my arms before I lose my footing fully.

"Shit. Thanks." I mutter, and he eases me onto the bed as I suck in a deep breath of fresh air.

Rummaging through his bag, he pulls out a bottle of water before cracking the lid. "Here."

I drink from it gratefully, then pass it back before he takes a sip.

"Thanks for inviting me," My words are slurred as I look at the moon through the window, and laughter erupts outside the door.

He shrugs as I glance lazily at him. "It was nothing." A flicker of something like guilt crosses his face, but it's so fleeting I'm not sure that I actually saw it.

The room spins some more and I take a deep breath. "Is being drunk always this... spinny?"

He laughs. "Oh yeah, it's your first time."

I nod, and he shifts on the bed. "Here, lying down might be easier, but leave a foot on the ground like this."

He leans over me, pushing my shoulders firmly as I lean backward. His hand hooks around the inside of my thigh, tugging my legs open until my right foot sits flat on the floor.

My mind is a mess, the world is still spinning albeit not as fast, and my body feels incredibly heavy.

Something's wrong.

"Oriana—" Seir's voice is a mixture of frustration and concern as it echoes in my mind.

It's okay. I'm just going to see if I can lay here for a while or sleep it off.

"Do not fucking fall asleep."

Why? It would be so easy to right now. I feel like a cloud. A heavy, spinning rain cloud.

"Fuck this."

The connection goes silent, leaving me alone with my thoughts as Liam's fingers trail gently up my thigh. "I'm glad you came tonight, Ori."

"This was fun," I manage to say, though it's difficult to form the words with my eyes threatening to roll back.

Did I really drink that much?

"I'll admit, I was kinda nervous to do this, but, they all assured me it would be easy if you just showed up."

Unease settles in my core, and I don't know if I'm imagining his hand pulling the skirt of my dress up. It's hard to tell with how numb and tingly my skin feels, but I know I'm not imagining it when he leans in to kiss my bare shoulder.

My mind races, and panic takes over. *Oh, god.*

I don't even know where my purse is to call 911.

A large part of me knows I wouldn't make it to my purse anyways. I can't move my body.

The world spins as my eyes roll back, and Liam's mouth trails down to my collarbone just as a loud bang echoes from downstairs. Shouting erupts, and loud, heavy footsteps thunder through the hallway before light casts into the room.

"It—it's not what it looks like!" Liam's voice is frantic, and it takes all my effort to turn my head toward the doorway.

Seir?

His hair looks damp, like he just got out of the shower only minutes ago. His chest heaves with his dress shirt half-buttoned, and a look of pure violence burns in his eyes as he stares at Liam which sends a shrill note that borderlines on excitement down my spine.

Seir says nothing as he takes long, confident strides toward the bed.

Liam panics, scrambling away. "I wasn't going to do anything! They dared me to get a video of her naked, that's it."

My blood runs cold as each word registers.

A prank. A dare. They never even wanted me here.

"They're irrelevant, Ori."

He bends down to the bed, pulling my dress lower to cover my thighs before scooping me into his chest. The water dripping from the hair falling over his forehead drops to my bare skin as he glares at Liam.

"Where's her purse?" His words are clipped, like he's just barely restraining himself as he tightens his grip on me.

Even with the cold droplets, my entire body feels flushed, and I don't know if it's from the alcohol, Seir, or embarrassment.

Liam sputters as he scrambles to the doorway. "Uh, it's, um, downstairs. I'll get it."

The room spins again, and I manage to lazily bring my hand to Seir's face, my fingertip tracing the stubble along his jawline before my hand falls into my chest.

Piercing blue eyes slide to mine, and even though the world spins with my mind in a haze, there's something keeping me glued to the present. It's as if his presence is sobering, yet equally intoxicating in his own way, and he turns to carry me down the stairs to the front door.

Hushed whispers and chatter follow us as Liam approaches Seir, holding out my purse.

"Take your purse from him."

Without hesitation, my heavy hand reaches out, grabbing the strap and pulling it into Seir's chest.

He's my lifeline right now.

I'd be a fool to think otherwise.

This is the second time he's gotten me out of a really bad situation.

He carries me down the driveway to a sleek black car with dark-tinted windows before opening the passenger door. Gently easing me into the seat, his hand curves protectively around my head until I'm settled.

Our faces are mere inches apart as he fastens my seatbelt, but I can't seem to tear my eyes off him even with the world spinning.

He suddenly shows up in my life, saves me from shitty situations twice, has powers and substitute teaches...

Who are you, Seir?

His gaze lingers on mine for a moment before he pulls away and shuts the door.

"That's a conversation for another day, Oriana Sharpe."

Ooo, my government name. Now I'm in trouble.

He pulls himself into the driver's seat, and the engine roars to life beneath us.

"Be thankful that Trouble is my second name."

I blink at him, and my words come out slurred. "Seir Trouble doesn't have a very good ring to it." I suck in a deep breath to try to get the rest out half-coherently. "Now, if it were Sir Trouble, then we're cooking with grease if you're some kind of knight."

He bursts out laughing, and I find myself smiling along with him as he backs out of the driveway and speeds off into the night.

Chapter 9

By the time we pull up to Rae's apartment, my stomach flips uneasily. I don't want to deal with her questions, and I'm not ready to be alone after what just happened.

"You won't be alone, Ori."

"I'm really never going to get used to this."

My words are still slurred, and it's hard to get them out even though my mind feels more clear than it was an hour ago.

Seir gets out of the car and walks to the passenger side door before leaning over me to unbuckle my seatbelt. I inhale the subtle scent of his woodsy cologne, feeling my body warm as he lifts me carefully into his arms. Kicking the door closed, he carries me up the steps and knocks twice at the door.

As much as I hate to admit it, there's a certain comfort in being this close to him, and I find myself leaning deeper into his chest as we wait at the door.

A soft repetitive thud of footsteps echo behind the door before it opens to Rae's wide eyes. "Oh my god, what happened? Mr. Harvard?"

She steps aside as he pushes past, walking straight to my room as if he's been here hundreds of times before kneeling next to my bed and setting me down on my back as a wave of unease churns my stomach.

"No," I say, shaking my head and jerking to sit up as he helps me, "Oh, no. Washroom."

I hurriedly hobble there with his help as Rae follows close behind us. Within seconds of brushing past the door, I fall forward to the ground. My knees slam to the floor in front of the toilet as hands pull my hair back, and I empty the contents of my stomach as tears pour from my eyes.

After a few torturous minutes, I reach up and fumble with the lever to flush the toilet as the sink faucet turns on. Within seconds, a damp cloth presses against the back of my neck and I release a deep sigh of relief.

This was such a fucking mistake.

"Yes. It was a large mistake. And I hate to tell you I told you so, but—"

I groan.

Don't dad me right now, please.

"I'm not—" his voice is cuts off by Rae, and I can almost picture her eyes as wide as saucers.

"Woah. Knowing about the telepathy thing is one thing, seeing it happen in person is a whole other ball game."

Pushing to my feet with Seir's arms bracing me, I take a deep breath and sway. "I would like for it to be known that I officially dislike alcohol, and I'm never drinking it again."

"And the lie detector determined, that was a lie." Rae giggles, handing me a glass of water, "There's a reason I avoid it. You'll feel worse in the morning."

Seir flashes us both a knowing grin, "Hmmm. Where have I heard that before?"

Ass.

His grin turns into a chuckle, and the room spins again.

"Ugh. I need to lay down."

"You need food."

I wave him off and shake my head. "No, no. I need sleep."

His jaw tightens, and he glances at the doorway. "Since you have Rae here, I really should get going."

"Yeah, isn't it kinda inappropriate for a professor to be around one of his drunk pupils?"

Seir just shrugs. "Worse things have happened."

My mind runs through the events of tonight, and dread washes over me as I realize the entire house saw Seir carrying me out of the house.

"It will be fine."

You won't get in trouble? I won't get in trouble?

The last thing I want is for him to lose his career and for me to be expelled. This college has the highest ratings for religious studies, psychology, and a few other degrees.

I don't want to mess anything up for either of us.

"I told you, it will be fine. Trust me."

He holds my gaze, and concede with a nod. "Alright."

"Man, I'm gonna need a warning before you guys start just looking at each other intensely like that. I didn't know whether you were gonna fight or fuck."

My eyes widen, and I turn to Rae as she grins from ear to ear.

Seir steps out the doorway, casting one last lingering glance at me before looking at Rae. "Take care of her tonight."

"Yes, sir." She replies with a grin and lazy salute, watching him disappear down the hall until the front door closes. She turns to me with a raised brow, but I just shake my head.

"Can I sleep in your room tonight?"

She nods, hooking my arm over her shoulder and escorts me down the hall to the stairs. "So what happened, Ori?"

I shake my head. "I'd rather not talk about it."

She falls silent the rest of the way up to her room, and by the time she leads me to the bed, my stomach is growling loud enough that it's impossible to ignore.

"Do you want—"

"Please."

She laughs quietly as she turns to the doorway, pausing halfway. "Leave it to you to be stubborn as hell when he said you needed food."

She's still laughing when she disappears around the corner, and I sigh deeply before falling backward onto the bed.

Maybe all of this was a mistake. This house, this school, this career choice.

My parents always wanted me to do something with the church, but I just couldn't bring myself to fit into the box they'd made for me.

With all their judgement, assumptions, punishments and threats... I thought counselling was a good choice.

I thought, if I could help someone who went through the same kind of trauma and challenges with rediscovering themselves, then maybe, just maybe, it might give me a purpose beyond just existing.

Sure, it might not be in the church like my parents wanted, but it still would be connective tissue to religion, and a way to serve others who are misguided like I was.

But now I don't know if it's something I want to do.

After tonight, I don't even know if I can face anyone at school again, let alone spend the next few years learning to trust people.

Maybe I should just get a job at some restaurant and start building my life from there.

"I heard sex work is another way to monetarily gain off serving others."

My cheeks burn.

Out of my head, teach.

He laughs, and the sound echoes through my mind as a ghost of a smile tugs at my lips.

"You can't seriously be considering quitting something you worked toward, and are passionate about, simply because of a few irrelevant meat sacks."

I choke on air as Rae comes walking back in, confusion etched across her face. "Uh, I don't know CPR so, you're on your own with this one if you're dying."

She hands me a peanut butter and jelly sandwich, and I grin at her before taking a bite. The salty and sweet flavors meld together, and I groan. "I always forget how good a PB&J is until I have one."

She giggles before crawling into bed, and I quickly down the sandwich before laying down alongside her.

"Hey Ori," She says, and my eyes find hers in the low moon light filtering in through the window.

"Yeah Rae?"

Her hand slides over to grasp mine. "Whatever happened today, will you promise me something?"

Emotion wells up in my throat and I nod, not trusting my voice.

"Promise me that you'll get them back for whatever happened tonight?"

I search her gaze, and I don't know that I can promise something like that to her. I don't even know who it was that dared him.

"I don't know how." My voice is hardly a whisper, and she just smiles at me, like it's the dumbest thing I've said in my entire life.

Which is impossible because I'm fully aware of the dumb things I actually have said to her before...

Like that time I told her I wanted to become a duck, so I can go quackers for crackers.

Seir's genuine laughter bursts out, and between him and the memory, I can't help but smile slightly.

"You know, the best way to get them back for whatever they did, is to see you succeed when they want you to fail."

I just stare at her from under the darkness of night, as the soft moonlight illuminates her features.

"Wise words, Rae."

"Damn straight. Tell Mr. Harvard I'm coming for his job."

Chapter 10

The next morning, birds chirp as the bed shifts, sending waves of pain radiating through my skull as I groan. "Ugh, this is the worst."

My stomach churns as Rae laughs. "I dunno, your breath might be arguably worse than your hangover."

I sit up and pain throbs in my head. "Why in the world would anyone do this more than once?"

She just cackles and disappears around the corner, her feet receding down the stairs before she returns again with a bottle of water in hand.

Downing its contents, she stares at me with wide eyes. "I've never seen someone demolish a drink that fast. You should be in a Hoover vacuum commercial."

I raise a brow at her as Seir's voice fills my mind.

"She has a point. Last night you downed three shots and an entire mixed drink in half an hour, while on an empty stomach. I'm surprised you're not more sick."

I roll my eyes, pushing to my feet as my stomach feels like it's shaking, and I unsteadily make my way down the stairs.

She follows me to the kitchen, grabbing an apple and washing it at the sink. "I work in an hour, are you gonna be okay here while I'm gone?"

"Yeah, I'm going to clean myself up and relax a bit to recuperate from last night."

"That's a good idea." She says with a nod before taking a bite of her apple. "Okay, I need to start getting ready or I'll be late."

She snags a napkin off the counter and walks back upstairs to change, leaving me alone with my thoughts as I vehemently avoid sorting through what happened at the party. I make my way to the washroom, choosing to instead reflect on Rae's advice from last night.

I know her logic was sound, and a large part of me wants to push forward without hesitation, but it's like the events that transpired threw my future map away, or put inverted signs on the roads I was travelling down for counseling.

The faucet squeals as I turn on the water and strip off my clothes.

What I want to do in essence hasn't changed, it's just that, the way I originally pictured getting my degree and moving into my career feels like it's suddenly been uprooted.

It's as if I can't see myself pushing through to the end of my education all because of what happened. My next steps feel so much more uncertain than they ever have been before.

I climb into the shower, slowly and mindlessly lathering the soap and shampoo over myself as I lose myself to my thoughts. By the time I'm finishing up my shower and toweling off, Rae's voice calls from the hallway.

"Ori! I'm leaving! See you later!"

"Drive safe!" My throat tightens as it always does when she leaves for work, and I swallow hard against the lump in it. Wrapping myself in a damp towel, I head to my bedroom to slip into jeans and a t-shirt, before I flop onto the bed.

My stomach churns uncomfortably again, and I groan.

"How's your head?" Seir's teasing voice sounds out, and I roll my eyes with a deep-seated sigh of resignation.

I'm not saying you were right.

"But..."

But I feel like absolute garbage.

"Well, lucky for you, I have just the remedy."

I frown as an engine rumbles outside before idling like someone just pulled up in front of the house.

He can't be...

Can he?

Are you outside?

"Aren't you perceptive? Yes. Now come, I have the perfect cure for a hangover."

A mixture of surprise and excitement washes over me, and despite feeling awful, I find myself more eager than I have been in months to leave the house. I grab my wallet from my purse and hurry to the front door, locking it behind me before walking to the dark mustang parked on the side of the road.

The horse logo on the front grill is different to those I've seen, with two large wings outstretched behind it and I raise a brow before pulling the passenger door open and peering inside.

Seir's hair is tousled as it falls forward, his leather jacket is a stark contrast to his normal suit and dress shirt, but still looks just as good on him.

I swallow as he flashes a knowing grin.

Don't even go there, Seir.

He lets out a genuine laugh, and I can't help the way my chest tightens before he shoots me a knowing look.

"Get in the car, Ori. We're curing that hangover."

I slide into the seat, and buckle myself in. "How exactly can you cure something this miserable?" I ask as he pulls away from the apartment with barely restrained humor painted on his features.

"When you say 'something this miserable,' do you mean you... or...?"

My jaw drops, and I blink at him as he just laughs harder.

"I'm glad someone is in good spirits."

He shrugs, but I don't miss the way his knuckles tighten on the wheel. "It's going to be a good day," he says before pointing a finger at me, "for both of us."

I huff a dry laugh and my head throbs, "Are we taking bets?"

He laughs again, turning onto a main road toward the highway. "That would hardly be fair."

My anxiety rises as the car speeds up quickly, the engine purring as it surges forward. "Do we have to go so fast?"

When I look at him, he's already glancing back at me with a scrutinizing expression. "Are they why you don't like to go fast?"

My heart races, and instead of easing off the gas, he speeds up to pass another car.

Oh my god, I'm going to hurl.

"Surprisingly, you aren't actually going to, but I think you need to address your fears."

My stomach flips as he passes another car and presses the pedal down further.

"Seir."

With my heart in my throat, and my blood pumping so hard I can hear it in my ears, I glance at the speedometer.

Holy shit, we were going one-thirty.

He eases off the accelerator after crossing three lanes in one swift movement before turning off a ramp and slowing down.

"I hate that you just did that, and I hate that you knew why it bothered me even more."

We come to a red light, and I can feel his gaze burning into the side of my head.

"Ori."

It takes a conscious effort to not turn to look at him as my pulse starts to calm down.

"Oriana."

The sudden command in his voice sends a shiver down my spine, and my eyes flick to his. He searches my face before reaching down to hook our pinkies together, and I blink at our hands.

"I promise that you are safe with me. You always will be."

The light turns green, and I pull my hand back into my lap. "You can't control other drivers."

He nods thoughtfully. "True, but I can control myself."

"Right. So why not just slow down?"

He laughs like the thought is absurd. "Because I don't need to."

Frustration simmers inside of me as he pulls into a parking spot, and instead of arguing further I just push it down before hurriedly unbuckling my seatbelt and getting out of the car.

"You're angry."

I shut the door and meet his gaze over the roof. His expression is one of genuine concern, as though he's really trying to understand.

I'm frustrated.

He glances around before closing the driver's side door and tilting his head as he looks at me.

"I nearly killed your professor to save your life, without physically being there, and you think a car crash is even possible, nevermind lethal with me beside you?"

The fierce look in his ocean-blue eyes is convincing enough, but I guess in my moment of anxiety I hadn't considered what he is capable of.

I only considered the risk.

Shaking my head, I move to the back of the car and wrap my arms around myself.

Sometimes in the chaos of everything, I forget that you are very much not normal.

He grins, stepping in close with his hand at the small of my back as he guides me toward the restaurant. We only get a few feet from the door when he leans in close, with amusement clear in his voice.

"Oriana Sharpe, you have no idea."

Chapter 11

We walk into the bustling restaurant, drawing some curious glances, though most people's attention lingers on Seir as we pass by.

I can't say I blame them.

Seir gestures to a nearby booth, and I ease into the cushioned seat as another pang radiates through my head. He must notice the scrunch of my face as he waves to a waiter walking by.

The man hurries over as he pulls out a notepad and a pen.

"Two waters, and two chili burgers with chili cheese fries please." Seir flashes the man a smile and the waiter just nods, scribbling down the order.

"Got it, that'll be out before you know it!" He says in a sing-song voice before hurrying to the back, and I blink, turning to look at Seir.

"Chili burgers? Chili cheese fries?"

He looks at me innocently. "What, you're not vegan are you?"

My jaw drops. "I was more concerned about the nutritional value."

His laugh is broad and infcctious as he leans back comfortably, angling himself toward me, "Trust me, you'll thank me later."

"Don't be so sure about that."

His grin just widens, as if he knows the world's biggest secret before his gaze scans the other tables.

"We will see." I murmur as the waiter comes back with our waters, placing them in front of us with a plate of lemon slices.

Squeezing the lemon, I plop it in the water before stirring and taking a grateful sip. One sip turns into two, and next thing I know, half the glass is gone.

He coughs a laugh and puts his water down. "Demolished indeed."

I meet his gaze, feeling oddly comfortable despite everything that's happened since we first met.

Is it because of everything that happened?

Or because of whatever this thing is that binds us together?

Perhaps both.

Putting my water onto the table, I lean back against the booth, "Has this ever happened to you before?"

He eyes me for a moment before shaking his head. "Never in my life."

And you have magic?

"May I say, you have rather embraced this method of communication quite well."

My cheeks burn as he smiles, covering his grin by taking a sip of water.

Well... I wouldn't want to be admitted again so soon. I fear hearing voices and talking about magic is grounds for another round of medication.

The muscle in his jaw flexes. "I'm sorry you went through that."

"It's in the past, hopefully."

So, magic.

His lips twitch. *"What do you want to know, eager little thing?"*

You've had abilities for how long?

The waiter brings over plates of food, setting four down in front of us as my mouth waters. The burgers are huge, with chili seeping out from the edges and a soft looking brioche bun on top covered in sesame seeds.

This is enough food for a small family.

"I've had my abilities all my life."

I blink, the distraction of food honestly nearly made me forget I even asked a question, and I lean forward to snag a bite of chili cheese fries.

To anyone else, it might just look like we're two people sharing a meal in relative silence, and the thought has me biting back a grin.

What do your abilities consist of?

He takes a bite of his burger nonchalantly as if we're not having the most bizarre conversation ever.

"If you knew, you would likely run screaming, accuse me of using them on you, or worse."

The admission makes my pulse hike, and I take another bite of fries, chewing them slowly if only to savor the cheesy deliciousness.

Tell me.

"No."

My head snaps to him. "Why?"

His eyes flick around before leveling on me, and the seriousness on his face sends a cold note of dread down my spine.

"I'm not ready for you to look at me for what I am."

I frown, searching his guarded expression with confusion.

The guy saved me twice when he hardly knows me, yet he thinks I will look at him differently simply because of what he's capable of?

It doesn't make any sense.

My eyes narrow on him.

Are you an alien?

He's mid-swallow when he chokes, sputtering and laughing as a smile tugs at the corner of my lips. I have to admit, there's a particular sense of satisfaction that comes with making him laugh.

"Alien. Oh, that's a good one. I don't think I've ever been asked that before."

My grin widens, and I lift the burger before taking a bite. The flavors fill my mouth and I groan.

You were right, this is intensely good. Why the hell is this so good?

"How's your stomach and headache?"

Still chewing, I pause thoughtfully. My head hasn't had the usual pang of pain since we arrived, and my stomach seems to be handling the food well.

Surprisingly better.

He gives me a smug look as I swallow the bite of food before taking a sip of my drink.

So do you have family?

He nods, taking another sip of his water.

"Huge family. One of those where you have no idea the actual number of siblings, and most of the ones you do know have gone off to do their own thing. You maybe hear from them once in a blue moon."

Sounds like aliens, Seir.

He smiles before taking a bite of fries, and it tightens my chest as my cheeks warm.

"Clearly I'm extra terrestrial."

Definitely extra.

I feel his gaze on me and glance at him, seeing amusement and something akin to feigned shock on his face, so I innocently take another bite of my food.

"Would you be amiable to come with me after lunch?"

Something inside me twists and flutters at the tentative hopefulness in his face. It's like he's outwardly confident, but equally uncertain of my reaction.

Still, something about him has really piqued my curiosity, and I can't help but want to spend more time with him. I still don't fully understand why this spell bound us together, and a large part of me feels like this is worth exploring more.

I nod and reach for another chili covered fry. "Sure. I don't think that'll hurt."

A smile graces his handsome features, and I can only hope that my trust isn't misplaced this time.

Not long after finishing lunch, we're turning off a main road into a residential area I've never been to before.

The houses are nice enough, but it's the large community center down the street that catches my attention. A handful of kids play basketball in the courtyard, with some watching and a worker or volunteer on the side directing the game.

We pull over on the side of the road as a couple heads turn our way, and when the engine cuts off, I look at Seir.

"A community center?" I ask with a frown as he scans the parking lot.

When his gaze slides to mine, he grins. "Children are the backbone of the future. Strengthening and being there for them is maybe the most important thing we can do in our lives."

I blink. I don't think I've ever heard anyone talk this kindly about children. "Are you certain you're not an alien?"

He laughs, and I can't help but smile with him as he unbuckles his seatbelt. "It's the truth. There's one kid here I've been coming to visit for the past few weeks every Saturday. Considering your aspirations, I thought you might want to talk with the counselor here."

My brows shoot up. "You would be okay with it?"

"It's the reason I asked for you to join. Perhaps this could help you make a decision for your future."

My chest tightens, for more reasons than one, and I open my mouth to speak when he raises his hand between us and wiggles his finger from side to side. "Ah, ah, ah. Don't thank me yet."

My mouth snaps shut, and I fight back a smile. "Okay, lead the way, Mr. Harvard."

He winces. "Have I told you I hate that name now?" he says, opening his door and standing up as I do the same.

I shake my head. "Nope. I honestly thought you liked it."

"Yeah, not at all."

He walks around the vehicle, and we pace to the front doors, pulling them open as cool air from the inside blasts us in a sudden rush. The moment we push past the doors into the main lobby, a squeal of excitement sounds out.

"Sir!" A little blonde-haired boy shrieks before running toward Seir. They go through a series of fist bumps, elbow knocks and high-fives as part of what I'm assuming is a secret handshake.

Sir, huh. Was I on the mark with you being a Knight, Sir Trouble?

Seir laughs outwardly. Whether it's due to my commentary or the excited child giggling at Seir's hand ruffling his hair, I'll probably never know.

"It's close enough."

My lips twitch as a middle-aged man steps into the doorway from one of the side rooms with a soft smile on his face. He leans his shoulder against the door frame and crosses his arms, watching the interaction between Seir and the little kid.

"Ben, this is Oriana. Oriana, this is Ben Harriot, one of the Licensed Professional Counselors here at the center."

Ben grins, putting a deep set of dimples on display. "I think you missed the word 'best' in that introduction."

Seir laughs. "Did I? How odd. Must be old age getting to me."

Both men break out into laughter before the young boy in front of Seir grasps his hand and starts pulling him into another room. "I made a picture for you!"

As they disappear through the doorway, I vaguely hear Seir's voice growing fainter as Ben takes a few steps closer until he's standing next to me, staring into the room with a look of contentment.

I don't know what to ask him.

There's a pause before Seir answers.

"Don't force it. Just have a conversation and it will come organically."

My mind races through possible questions to ask, but thankfully Ben breaks the silence first. "He's the happiest when Seir visits, you know."

My chest tightens. "They seem like they've formed quite the bond."

Ben nods, but the sad smile on his face as his eyes lock with mine makes me question everything I assumed about the small cheerful child.

"Before they met, Seir would come every few weeks to make sure we had things we need around the center, but one weekend Seir stopped by while Vincent was here. Vincent was growing increasingly withdrawn and none of us could get through to him."

I tear my gaze from Ben to look at the doorway as he continues, "Seir took one look at Vince, and it was like the entire world stopped existing. He visited daily for a week. The moment I texted him to say Vince was here, it was hardly half an hour before he showed up."

There's a long pause before he continues, "Whatever he did in that week helped Vince open up more about what was happening in his life that was making him withdraw into himself. I still will never understand how, but I'm damn thankful he did."

The lump in my throat grows, but I glance at Ben before asking. "What was making him withdraw?"

Ben gives me a sad smile, his brows twitching inward as if the thought is painful, "He lost his mother a few months ago, and his father started seeing a new woman pretty quickly afterward. She heavily relies on punishment to teach aversion to what she considers bad behaviors."

He crosses his arms over his chest, and Vince's laugh rings out in the distance, "One of the hardest things for Vince was that she would call him a demon and evil for struggling to adjust to these changes and the new normal. She told him that he was going to go to Hell for being so difficult. The poor child was still coping with the loss of his mother, I don't blame him for acting out when he doesn't know how to express what he's feeling."

I nod, feeling like I might understand Vince more than anyone has any right to. "How has he been coping recently?"

Ben's smile widens like this is the best part of the entire situation, "He's been doing great. He still has bad days, but he no longer thinks he is the reason his mother died, he doesn't blame himself, and he has gained a lot of self-esteem. He even started to draw again which is something he hadn't done since he lost his mother."

Vince shrieks into a laugh as Ben and I smile at one another.

"But enough about problems of the past. What about you, Oriana?"

I let out a genuine laugh. "Trying to get in my head already, huh?"

Ben's jaw drops before he grins. "I would never."

"When he says he'd never, just know it's the opposite," Seir's voice rings out as Vince leads him into the room by hand.

"Ah, back so soon?" Ben grins as Vince takes off toward the courtyard in a full sprint.

"He just wanted to show me his drawings today and then said he wanted to play basketball with Mark soon. He seemed very adamant he was going to win." Seir's looks between us. "Sorry if we interrupted."

Ben's hands wave dismissively. "No, no, we were just about to dive into the mysteries of Oriana."

Seir's grin widens as his gaze finds mine. "There are quite a few mysteries there indeed." My cheeks burn. "She actually is interested in your line of work, Benny." He says, jabbing his elbow toward Ben's arm jokingly.

"Oh really?"

I nod. "Yes, currently going to school for it."

Ben's eyes light up like a kid on Christmas morning. "What made you want to come into my neck of the woods?"

I give him a soft smile, glancing in the direction Vince ran off only minutes before. "For stories like Vincent's."

Chapter 12

By the time we're in the car again, the sun is in its descent from the sky, and I yawn deeply.

I ate more today than I have in weeks. I feel more certain about my choices for the future than I ever have, and most, if not all of it is due to Seir.

He may have shown up like a whirlwind into my life through an egregiously unconventional method, but I can't help but appreciate everything that has come with his arrival.

Settling into my seat and buckling my seatbelt, I glance at Seir as he gets comfortable in the driver's side. "I know you stopped me earlier, but thank you for all of this."

He clicks his seatbelt on and tilts his head, his piercing ocean blue gaze searching my face. "You never have to thank me for anything, Oriana. You deserve happiness, and you deserve to choose your path in life without having assholes who think they're better than others ruin that for you."

I offer him a soft smile. "Is Vince getting that same message too? Cause it sure seems like it's worked for him."

A smile graces his features, but there's only bitterness and sadness behind it. "Religion is not what most people think it is. The devil is real, but he exists in a place where he doesn't belong. Religion is a war, Oriana, and love will be the only way we reach salvation. Vince just had to realize that his love for his mother and father did not make him the enemy. Words and art could be his outlet rather than his isolation, and his existence does not make him evil."

I swallow, struggling to absorb everything he said. "Here I thought Rae was the wise one."

He grins, and my stomach flips chaotically. "Feel free to reserve that judgement for later," he says, putting the car into drive before pulling away from the community center.

It's a comfortable silence as we drive home, and I'm lost in thought, reminiscing on the events of today when we turn onto the familiar street of Rae's house.

An ounce of dread pools in my gut, and I shove it away.

I can't really be this unhappy that we're about to say goodbye for the night, can I?

Grappling with my thoughts, I'm snapped back into reality as he pulls over and parks along the side of the road. "Ori," he says as I unbuckle my seatbelt, and I hesitate before raising my gaze to his.

He tilts his head, and as his dark hair falls to the side over his eyes, I notice the curve of his lips, and the softness in the way he's looking at me makes something flutter in my chest as his lips part.

"Yes?" I say, my voice coming out more breathless than intended.

His lips twitch for a flicker of a moment before turning more serious, "Thank you for coming with me today."

I swallow and nod. "Thank you for having me, Seir."

His eyes flash with an emotion I can't quite place, and I open the door with a click.

If I don't go inside now, I'm not sure that I ever will.

"You say that like it's a bad thing."

My cheeks burn, and I shoot him a look through the window as he smiles.

Ass.

"I did nothing wrong."

I hear his laugh from inside the car as I walk away, biting back the ghost of a smile that's fighting its way forward as I reach the door.

I've hardly gotten my key out when the door flies open, and Rae's figure fills my vision as she throws her hands on her hips.

I cover my mind again, hoping that it gives me a little privacy for the millions of questions I'm about to receive in this interrogation.

"Where were you?!" She demands, eyeing Seir's car on the side of the road before looking at me with a raised brow. "Are you boning our college professor now?!"

My jaw drops, and I step inside, shutting the door quickly behind me.

Who knows, maybe he has supersonic hearing or something.

"I am not boning him."

She shoots me an incredulous look. "I've told you before you are a terrible liar, and I can tell, once again, that you're lying to me, Ori."

I blink and my brows pinch together. "No, I'm actually not. Seriously."

Her eyes narrow on me, and she grasps my hand before leading me to the front room where she sits me down. "Then why do you have this look on your face like you just, I dunno, made out with someone or fell in love?"

My pulse hikes.

I can't deny something has changed today.

Every inch of him makes my body react in a way I can't fully comprehend. It was one thing to acknowledge my physical attraction to him when I first saw him in class, but after today, it's as if I've seen him in an entirely different light.

"I don't know, Rae. We didn't do anything, honestly. We went for lunch, and then he brought me to a community center to speak with a counselor there."

"Like to get you evaluated or---?"

I laugh genuinely, and she stares at me like she has never seen me before. "Oh my god, Ori."

My laughter quiets, and I frown at her. "What?"

"Just, tell me you'll use protection."

My jaw drops again. "Rae!" I say with a strangled laugh. "It's not like that!"

"Right, well, just remind me of this moment when it happens."

I roll my eyes sarcastically before tossing her a grin. "Sorry if I worried you."

She blinks at me, and her face contorts as if she just remembered the entire reason she was angry. "You better be! I came home thinking you were abducted. We need to get you a new phone."

I wince. "Yeah, maybe in a few weeks. I'll suffer with this one for now."

"That one sucks, its ringer never worked half the time and it hardly got service."

I shrug, lifting the cover over my mind. "It's better than nothing."

Rae eyes me with scrutiny before turning toward the television, "Well let's watch some TV at the very least... You look like you could use a distraction... or a vibrator."

I blink at her and wave my hands in the air. "Nope. TV shows only, lets go," I say loudly, snatching the remote and flicking it on as she leans back on the couch, eyeing me with a smug look on her face.

The issue is that I can't exactly disagree with what she's saying. Not after today.

After a handful of episodes of stand-up comedy, I yawn deeply. "I need to sleep Rae, I'm tired as hell." I whisper, glancing over to see her already asleep against the other arm of the couch.

Pulling the blanket from the back cushion, I cover her with it and flick the television off before quietly padding my way to my bedroom.

I get to the doorway when my pinky toe suddenly collides with the corner, and my mouth drops open in a silent scream.

Oh, fuck. Fuck me.

Oh, god that hurt.

Oh, fuck, shit, fuck.

"Quite a colorful vernacular there."

Have you ever stubbed your toe, Mr. Magic man? Because if you haven't, let me tell you, it's the equivalent of having your foot torn off, burned and then put back on.

"I—"

And then once it's put back on, it's sawed off with dental floss, okay?

"I'm concerned about your experiences with stubbing your toe, because that description doesn't quite match what I have felt."

Pain radiates in my toe up to my heel as I hobble over to my bed.

I think I broke it.

"Do you need me to come check?"

My entire body flushes.

Second thought, my toe is fine.

He laughs, and the sound sends my mind into a tailspin as I pull off my jeans and t-shirt before throwing myself into bed in my underwear. I lay there for a long moment, staring at the way the moonlight casts shadows into the room before pulling the blankets over my body.

A shiver runs down my spine, and I pull the blankets higher.

Hey, Seir?

Part of me knows I should go to sleep, but the other part of me craves interactions with him like nothing else I've ever experienced. Each one giving me a high as good as the last but once it wears off, I'm fiending for more.

"Yes, Oriana?"

My heart pounds, the temperature of my body rises, and my palms get clammy beneath the sheets as I wrap my arms around my body.

Are you okay with us being able to hear one another like this?

A long moment passes, and the wind howls against the window as it rattles quietly.

"Why wouldn't I be?"

Well clearly this isn't normal to have someone in your head... I just wanted to make sure you're okay with it.

"Are you asking me if I'm okay with the connection between us or if I'm okay with the connection being with you?"

My pulse thunders and my nerves skyrocket.

I guess both.

"There has not been a moment since we connected that I have had any negative inclination to what's between us."

When he pauses, I don't know whether he's done talking or not, and conflict wars within me when I consider breaking the silence, but he finally speaks.

"Outside of being curious as to how and why this happened, and wanting to uncover the meaning behind it, I have no reservations in saying that I actually have enjoyed our conversations—probably more than I have any right to—and should the day ever come where this connection is severed, I will detest it."

I swallow hard, nodding even though he can't see me.

Me too, Seir.

"Get some sleep, Oriana Sharpe."

Heat rises to my cheeks as I turn over to my side, and my eyes slide shut.

Goodnight, Seir.

Chapter 13

The next morning my eyes peel open to the sound of birds chirping, and the quiet patter of rain against the window. Stretching, I feel several bones pop and groan.

I'm not even in my mid-twenties yet, and I sound like I'm going to break if I get out of bed the wrong way.

Footsteps sound out down the hall and my door flies open. "Oriana!"

I blink as Rae's loud singsong voice fills the air, and she places a bag in front of me on the bed.

"Why are you this awake this early?" I croak and fall backward onto the bed in a huff.

"Early? You slept in. It's literally one o'clock in the afternoon, and I got home an hour ago from shopping."

She went without me!?

I open my mouth to speak, staring at her in disbelief as she plops down beside me, wiggling her finger between us.

"Ah! Not clothes shopping, we can do that some other time. I went toy shopping for you, because I knew there was no way in hell you'd go on your own or come with me."

My eyes widen at the suggestive logo on the bag, and the realization sinks in. "Rae! I do not need any toys!"

She just grins like she knows everything I'm saying is a damn lie.

"You don't have to use it right now, but like, for a rainy day." She glances out the window. "Oops, well. Another rainy day maybe."

It's all I can do to stare at her, and the moment my gaze drops to the bag, she excitedly inches it closer.

"Go ahead. Check it out!"

Sitting up, I put my hand into the bag and groan. "I can't believe you."

Her laugh fills the air, and she leans onto one arm. "You love me anyways though. And you'll probably love me more after you use it."

I roll my eyes and pull a large box out of the bag. The image on the box is a silicone rose vibrator and heat rises to my cheeks.

"Well this is an unexpected surprise."

Panic rifles through me, and I pull the cover over my mind before throwing the box to the bed with a thud.

Oh, god.

Oh, my fucking god.

I cover my face and groan, hearing the concern in Rae's voice. "Oh no, you hate it. I can take it back."

Waving my hands between us, I shake my head. "No, it's not that. I just... I had an audience." When I peer at her from between my fingers, she takes one look at my face before bursting out laughing.

"Well, at least that breaks the ice a little."

Groaning, I fall backward onto the bed as she takes the empty bag and walks to the doorway.

"There's lunch in the fridge if you want!" She says between fits of laughter, and my face burns even more.

I can never show my face to him again.

Officially.

I'm about to lift the cover off my mind when my hand lands on the box, and I sigh deeply. I might as well open it first.

By the time I've lifted the silicone device from the packaging, my heart feels like it could beat out of my chest. Not only have I never used a toy before... but I've never seen anything quite like this in my life.

Placing it on the side table, I plug the charger into the wall, and connect the two magnetic charging pieces to the side of it as an LED light blinks in response.

Right. Well. There's that. Here's to self-love, I guess.

I turn and walk out the door, lifting whatever meager cover I had off my mind before padding to the kitchen. Rae is sitting at the table, putting on her makeup, and I frown.

"Working tonight?"

She shakes her head. "Date. I met this guy from work and he asked me out. He's in a rock band." She tosses me a wink. "Besides, you seem like you could use a night to... unwind."

I roll my eyes. "I guess it's a movie night for me."

Pausing with her mascara brush in her hand, she glances at me. "You seriously just need some time to relax, Ori. You've been through hell recently. Just enjoy the night. Make some popcorn, get a soda and binge-watch some movies."

Pulling a to-go container from the fridge, I bring it to the table and sit in front of her. "That doesn't sound half bad, actually."

She finishes applying her mascara before putting it into the tube, and I'm taking a bite of a wrap as she eyes me carefully.

"What?" I ask, frowning as she puts her mascara in her bag.

The look she's giving me is like she's trying to decide whether she should say something or not, and I sigh.

"Just say it, Rae. You can't give me that face and leave me hanging."

"It's just..." She hesitates, bringing her hands into her lap and pursing her lips. "Ori, you went months without eating regularly, and there was some weeks where I maybe saw you eat twice. Since meeting Mr. Harvard, you've just seemed... more you."

My chest tightens and I take another small bite of my wrap. "Are you saying that's bad?"

She shakes her head. "No. Not at all. It's just an observation more than anything. I just hope it stays this way."

She pauses before picking up the rest of her makeup and placing it into her bag. By the time she's done, it's been a long moment, and she unties her hair as she goes to stand up.

"You look beautiful, Rae." I stand to give her a hug, and she wraps her arms around me.

"Thank you," She whispers into my hair, and I lean the side of my head against hers.

"Sisters." I say quietly, and I feel her nod slightly.

"Sisters."

Chapter 14

By the time she leaves, it's nearly six o'clock, and a nervous excitement brims inside of me as I tug my pillow off the bed and hoist it into the front room.

I feel like a little kid left alone for the first time.

Plopping my pillow onto the couch, I snag the remote and start flipping through movie channels. The ending to a romantic comedy catches my attention, and I toss the remote to the couch before making my way to the kitchen.

It's not long before I'm returning to the front room with popcorn and a drink in hand when I sit down comfortably with a contented sigh.

As some cheesy comedy movie plays, I pick up the remote again and flip through channels, pausing for a few seconds on a horror movie with suspenseful music.

"That one looks promising."

A smile tugs at my lips.

You would want a horror movie. Sorry, no alien vs predator tonight.

His laughter sounds out, bleeding into me as I giggle to myself softly before flipping through to the next movie.

Another comedy.

"Pass."

My brows shoot up.

Excuse me, this is my movie night.

"*Are you kicking me out again?*"

Again?

He chuckles, and my cheeks heat.

"*Am I not permitted to join movie night?*"

I suck my tooth nervously before clicking my tongue.

Fine. You can stay.

It's not like I was going to deny him otherwise. I flip through, and land on a corny horror movie released a couple of decades ago.

"*Really? This one?*" His voice drips with feigned exasperation.

What's wrong with a classic?!

"*I thought you had better taste, Ori.*"

My eyes roll, and I flip the channel again as he laughs.

Bully.

I finally land on Scary Movie and I can almost hear the smile on his face.

"*Oh, good choice. Now this, this is a classic I can get behind.*"

A quarter way through the movie, Seir's sigh sounds out in my mind.

Everything okay?

There's a long pause, and I take a bite of popcorn as a funny scene flashes across the screen.

"*Yeah, Ori. I'm alright.*"

He sounds almost sad, and it's so unlike him that I frown.

Tell me.

Silence stretches between us, and I look away from the television altogether.

"*It's just been many, many years since I've—*"

His voice cuts off, and I feel like I'm hanging on a ledge. Like his next words could make or break me. My heart thunders with each passing moment that feels like an eternity until I finally get fed up with waiting.

Since you've what?

There's a moment of silence still before he responds.

"Since I've felt this happy."

I frown slightly at the minimalistic answer.

*Are you sure **you** don't need a counselor, Seir?*

He laughs softly.

"You up for the job?"

I don't know, you seem like you're a lot to handle.

The dark chuckle that echoes into my mind sends a cold shiver down my spine.

"You have no idea, Oriana."

My gaze flicks to the screen, and my cheeks burn as couples kiss in the back seat of a moving car. My mind instantly goes back to when Seir dropped me off, and my heart pounds in my chest.

Shit.

"My turn, are you alright?"

I laugh awkwardly, shoving away the mental image.

Oh yeah, just peachy.

"If I'm making you uncomfortable I can go."

His voice is half teasing, half serious, and my heart drops. I shake my head even though he can't see me.

No, I'd like for you to stay.

"Are you sure?"

Please.

"Please, what?"

The teasing in his voice has grown, and my cheeks burn. I feel out of breath, yet all I've done is sit here and stare at the screen, not paying any attention to the movie solely because of Seir.

Please stay.

"Well, considering I could never deny you anything, I'll stay."

My lips twitch slightly, and I suppress a laugh.

Can't deny me anything?!

"Nope. I've been completely at your mercy since we met."

The laugh that escapes me is genuine and my hand moves to cover my mouth.

You're funny.

"What's funny is that you think I'm joking."

My brow raises in disbelief as he just laughs dryly, and I'm nearly convinced as I grab the remote, flicking the television to the next channel absentmindedly.

The scene is a couple passionately kissing in bed, and my heart races.

Have you ever been in love before?

I don't even know where the question came from, or why I asked it without any warning or hesitation, but I find myself holding my breath as I wait for his answer.

"Love comes in many different forms, Oriana, and I've always been convinced that it comes with pain, or sacrifice. When it comes to the true love people read about or see in movies? The kind where you fit into one anothers world, where it hurts to breathe without them, and you would bring about the end of the world if it just meant one more minute together... In the years I've been alive, I have thought it impossible to find something that upends my world like those stories and films portray."

His words sink in, and I frown. The way he talks is like love is conditional, and I swallow hard at the recognition of how that feels.

Do you think you deserve to find that kind of love?

There's a long moment of silence between us, but I wait. He has to know he's worthy of it. Even in the short time I've known him, everything I've seen of him has lcd me to believe he's good. Even if my first experience was him nearly killing someone, he did it to save me.

"That may be for God to decide."

Frowning, my gaze flicks to the television again as the couple moves in sync. The look on her face is that of ecstasy as her nails dig into him, and my first instinct is to look away, but I don't.

I watch as the man on screen clutches her close, her eyes roll back, and they pant before kissing once again.

I don't think God should control that kind of thing, and you are worthy of it, even if you do not think so.

The woman on the screen pants as they continue to kiss one another, and part of me starts to wonder if this is what all couples experience when Seir chuckles slightly.

"It's always humorous how the film industry terribly captures what true intimacy is like."

I blink.

In what way?

"She looks satisfied. Most men are disappointing at best."

How motivational. At least you said most.

Laughter sounds out, and I laugh under my breath with him before releasing a deep yawn.

Say, how old is an alien like you anyways?

"Far too old to count."

I laugh, but the lack of humor on his end has my own dying on my lips as I process what he said. Oddly enough, I don't find that I have any sort of negative reaction to his age.

Perhaps because to me, he just feels like Seir. He doesn't act as though he's millennia old.

I mean, what does it matter anyways, it's not like we're together.

My gaze flicks to the television again. The man on the screen shoves the woman against a wall, his hand wraps her throat and my heart thunders in my chest.

So what is real intimacy like then?

His voice sounds tight as he responds.

"It's raw. It's selfish and selfless at the same time. Like needing to be close enough that your soul burns but wanting to savor every moment and draw it out as long as possible. It's knowing that at any second the world could come crashing down around you both, but

that pales in comparison to the thought of ending of what you've begun."

I swallow at the emotions thick in my throat. He sounds like he's speaking from experience, but I don't have the heart or guts to ask.

That sounds like love.

"Perhaps it is."

I yawn and flip off the television, grabbing my pillow before walking to the bedroom.

"I'll let you rest."

Stay.

"I—"

Unless you would prefer to leave, please stay.

"You know, there was once a time, I think you were relieved when I was silent."

A smile tugs at my lips as shut the door behind me, pulling my t-shirt overhead before tossing it into the laundry basket. Tugging my pants off, I plop my pillow down before crawling under the covers.

That was before I knew you were real, and I wasn't crazy.

"Are you certain on the crazy part?"

Fair point.

He laughs, and I lay flat on my back, staring at the dancing shadows as the wind blows outside.

Do you trust me enough yet to tell me what your powers are?

"Still stuck on that, are you?"

I shrug.

It makes me curious.

I can hear the smile in his voice as he speaks.

"Would it terrify you to know that I can show you glimpses of your future?"

My eyebrows shoot up.

Lies.

"I would not lie about that, least of all to you."

The admission warms my body, and I swallow.

Want to show me something?

"Depends what you want to see."

Surprise me.

His voice lowers, and my stomach flips.

"Your wish is my command. Shut your eyes."

My lids flutter closed as a quiet buzzing sound fills their air, followed by a gasp, and an image forms on the back of my eyelids of me writhing in bed. My skirt is hiked around my waist, and my hand between my legs makes my entire body warm. I watch my legs twitch as I pant, my back arches before my eyes snap open toward the closet and I freeze when the vision suddenly disappears.

Oh my god.

I'd say there's no way that's real, but part of me knows exactly what was happening, and my heart pounds like I've just run a mile.

"Anything else you'd like to see?"

The heat in his voice is thick, and it sends my own pulse raging as desire builds in my core.

Seir.

"Hmm?"

Could you see it too?

"Yes."

Was I—?

"What do you think?"

Oh, god.

"I don't think God had any part in that."

This is so embarrassing.

"No, it is not."

My cheeks burn, and I shake my head.

You know as well as I do what was happening there, Seir.

"And?"

And? What do you mean, and?

"There's nothing wrong with that."

But I was---

I can't verbalize it. It's too personal.

"Luckily for you, Oriana Sharpe, I'm inside your head. You don't need to verbalize anything for me to know what's going on in your mind."

A tingle glides along my cheek and I inhale sharply.

"Close your eyes."

Why?

"Close."

The authority in his voice makes my pulse jump, and I squeeze them shut.

"Open."

My gaze flicks in the direction of his voice to where he stands at the foot of my bed, and my chest heaves.

"How did you—?"

Even in the low moonlight, I see his brow raise like I should know the answer to that question, and he strides alongside the bed. The last time he was in my bedroom was the night I was drunk, and I am viciously wishing I had liquid courage as he crawls over me, the bed shifting slightly with his movement.

I don't dare to breathe as he hovers himself inches above me, looking into my eyes from the shadows.

"You wanted to know more of my abilities." His lips twitch slightly, as if I'm getting exactly what I asked for.

I am, and he absolutely knows it.

My heart stutters, and my stomach flips as his eyes drop to my mouth. "Tell me what you want, Oriana."

Breathing his air is intoxicating. The faint scent of his woodsy cologne with everything that is **him** in my vision sends a heady dose of desire into my veins as my hands grip the sheets tight.

My mind wanders to the movie, to the proposed false scene of intimacy as Seir called them, and my mouth drops open.

Before I can voice it, he leans in to brush his lips against mine. The action is so light, so minimal, but it's like everything in me screams to close the distance.

So I do.

The moment I lean forward, our lips touch, and the desire inside of me rages like an inferno. My mind is a whirlwind of emotions as his lips dance against mine.

By the time we break apart, my chest is heaving, and my body craves more, but he pulls away. His piercing blue eyes search mine as if looking for some answer before he presses another soft kiss against my lips.

His voice is no more than a whisper as he presses his head to mine. "What are you doing to me, Ori?"

My chest tightens at the pained tone to his hushed words, and I don't have time to ask before his lips crash against mine. When my hands finally lift off the bed, aching from how hard I've been gripping the sheets, I pause abruptly.

My eyes snap open to my empty room, and I blink in confusion.

What—?

Did I do something wrong?

Was that a dream?

"It wasn't a dream. I never should have done that to begin with."

Oh.

My stomach flips uneasily, and I wrap my arms around myself, still not believing what just happened.

I'm sorry if I–

"Oriana, it's nothing you did."

Then what–

"If I stayed any longer, we would not have been able to stop."

Part of me wants to ask more questions, but the other part of me knows what I just experienced was a lot to take in itself.

I don't know whether I'm disappointed or relieved.

Do you regret it?

There's a long pause before he answers, and his voice is gentle, like a soft caress as it echoes through my mind.

"Not in a million lifetimes."

Chapter 15

After a long, restless night, I wake to the sound of my alarm with an odd mixture of contentment and nervousness.

"Wakey wakey sleepyhead!" Rae's voice rings out, and I groan at how happy she sounds first thing in the morning.

She opens the door and peers in as I sit up, "What time did you get home?"

Padding into the room, she grins. "Like two o'clock or so." she raises her palms between us as my eyes widen. "Relax, nothing happened. We just lost track of time."

My eyes narrow on her. "That's also what you'd say if something happened."

She shrugs. "Maybe, but this time I'm serious. His family is like your parents, so staying up late was fine, but there was no way in Hell—literally—that we were going to do anything more than talk."

I laugh quietly, and she grimaces. "Sorry, I didn't mean to mention them."

"It's fine."

Truth be told, even though I miss them and my old life, things have gotten easier. I don't think I'm ready to speculate why that might be, even though I think I already know the answer.

"Come on, you slept in and snoozed your alarms twice. We gotta go."

I glance at the time on Rae's phone and wince. "Damn. Okay give me a minute, I'll be right out."

She closes the door behind her, and I go to unplug my phone as my gaze falls on the rose toy on the bed table. Memories of last night flood back, and my pulse quickens.

I move to the dresser, glancing in the mirror as my heart pounds steadily in my chest. The way I look makes my throat constrict with emotion.

My cheeks aren't as sunken in, the dark bags under my eyes have all but disappeared, and my skin just overall looks more taken care of and soft.

It's like in the short time I've known Seir, he's managed to tip over the whirlwind of a spiral I was going down, flipped it around so much so that I'm finally starting to look more like myself again after months.

I dress quickly before using the washroom and brushing my teeth. As much as I'd like to shower, there's just no time.

Rae gives me an exasperated, but hopeful look as I reach the front door. "I was starting to wonder if you were going to just call it in today."

I shake my head.

After what happened at the party, I'm dreading going, but it's necessary. The more I avoid uncomfortable situations, the less I'll be able to handle them.

"Not a chance," I say with a grin, hooking my arm in hers and tugging her out the door.

We keep a brisk pace to make up time, and as we're a block away from campus, I glance over at Rae's thoughtful features.

"So do you like this guy?"

She blinks, looking at me with a bashful nod. "I think so. It's hard cause we just met, but he seems nice."

The thought reminds me of what Seir said about true love and how most men are disappointments as my eyes flick from her to our path.

I can't help but hope that he's not one of the disappointing ones.

"So, what about you and Mr. Harvard?" She whispers as we cross the street towards the building where other students are filing in.

I shake my head, "It's... complicated."

"Yeah, you think? That's why I'm asking. What are you going to do?"

I frown. "What do you mean?"

She grips my arm and stops us at the bottom of the entrance steps. Her gaze darts around as she whispers more quietly than I've ever seen her do before.

"I'm not blind, Ori. I can see there's something there. Whoever he is, he cares more than he lets on, and same with you. You're both like two planets orbiting one another as gravity slowly pulls you in. You're going to collide at some point, so what are you going to do when that happens?"

I blink at her.

If only she knew.

"Why don't you tell her?"

My cheeks burn, and she sees my reaction before wincing. "Oh, he heard that didn't he?"

I nod, and she hooks our arms together again, leading us up to the entrance.

You want me to tell her that you teleported into my room last night?

"I want you to do what you're comfortable with, and you don't like keeping secrets from her. But if you are going to tell her, you're going to tell her the whole truth—in that I only did so in a desperate attempt to satiate my own selfish needs."

My heart stutters in my chest as my pulse hikes.

And what selfish needs were those?

"To feel your skin against mine again, to taste you on my tongue and to have you beneath me."

So you're satiated, then?

"Not yet."

Desire pulsates in my body, and butterflies flit chaotically in my chest. It takes a conscious effort to stay focused as Rae leads us to class.

How the hell am I going to get through an hour in a room with him?

His chuckle sounds in my mind, and I blow out a breath as we round the last corner. Groups of students have collected outside the class with the group whispering to one another near the door.

At the center of the group next to the wall is Liam. He does a double-take before a mixture of guilt and worry paints his features.

"Ignore them, Ori."

I swallow hard, forcing myself to keep pace with Rae as their murmurs follow us.

The moment I step into the room, my eyes slide to Seir's tall form standing by his desk. He's leaning back on the edge of the dark, solid wood with his piercing blue eyes scanning the room before they lock onto me.

He tracks my movements, and I force myself to look away to avoid stumbling as I make my way to my seat. His gaze burns into my skin as I ease into my chair, with Rae taking the desk next to mine.

She glances between the front of the room and me, then leans in to whisper, "Uh Ori, he's—"

"I know."

More students file in, and I chance another look toward the front desk to see him still staring at me.

My entire body feels like it's radiating heat, and I'm nearly certain I've turned a shade of red never seen before.

They're going to notice.

"And?"

I don't think it's a good look for a professor to be staring at a stu-dent like he wants to eat her.

His lips twitch, and he—albeit reluctantly—tears his gaze away to address the rest of the class.

"I couldn't care less how it looks, but since it bothers you..."

My stomach flips as Rae scooches closer. "What's he saying?"

My eyes widen as I glance at her, and her face is a mixture of pure curiosity and excitement.

"I'm not even going there." I hiss back, and she giggles as I force my attention from gravitating to the front of the room.

Chapter 16

The last of the students settle into their seats, and Seir's eyes linger on a pale Liam before he speaks. "Hope you all had a restful weekend, because today we're going to be diving into demonology. Can anyone tell me where the word demon derived from?"

Lucille in the front raises her hand, and Seir nods at her. "Go on."

"It comes from the Greek word daimōn."

"Good. Who can tell me what daimōn means?"

Kyle raises his hand, and Seir acknowledges him with a gesture before Kyle's shaky voice responds. "It means spirit, deity or a supernatural entity?"

Seir's lips twitch. "Are you asking me? You don't sound certain."

Kyle's head shakes. "No, sir. I'm just... There was just a few translations of it, that's all."

Sir Trouble.

My lips twitch as Seir's gaze flicks in my direction.

"Ms. Sharpe. Can you tell me what three classes of daimōns exist within theology, occultism and religious doctrincs?" He clicks his tongue as I blink at him.

Ass.

"Non-human, discarnate entities, and separated souls, sir."

His eyes flash at the last word to leave my lips and a chill shoots down my spine.

"Good work, Ms. Sharpe. Now, referring back to our conversation last week, are all daimōns evil? Liam... why don't you answer this one?"

Liam pales even further as Seir stares down at him, almost in challenge.

You don't have to---

"He will answer the question."

Liam frowns. "I can't answer that question."

Seir flashes a smile at him. "Why is that?"

"What I've been taught---"

His mouth snaps shut as Seir holds his palm out between them. "Quite frankly, I do not care what you've been taught up to this point. What did the booklet I handed out to everyone **teach** you about whether demons are evil?"

Liam shifts uncomfortably, "Respectfully---"

Seir launches off the edge of the desk and slams his hands down on top of Liam's desk with a bang, making everyone jump. His eyes burn with a level of anger I've never seen before, and Liam swallows.

"Do not speak as if you know what the word respect means. Now answer the God-damned question."

Liam's voice wavers as his hands tremble against his desk. "N-n-no, sir. Th-they aren't all e-evil."

Seir grins and straightens, tilting his head before he glances around the room.

"Told you, he would answer."

"That is correct. Many entities considered to be demons are actually neutral, in contrast to their often malevolent portrayal in various cultures–or as you would put it, evil."

He walks to the board at the front of the class, marking one, two, three and four all on different rows before pointing to the first one.

"We have classified demons as spirits of varying kinds. Depending on the culture, this can mean different things. Given its prevalence, we'll start with Christianity. What are demons in Christianity?"

Luke puts his hand up quickly, and Seir raises a brow but points at him. "Demons in Christianity are fallen angels who tempt humans to sin." Luke practically sneers the words out, and I notice Seir's jaw tense.

"What is a fallen angel, Lucas?"

Luke blinks, straightening in his chair. "An angel who has sinned, Mr. Harvard."

"That fucking name again."

My lips twitch with suppressed laughter as Seir writes "angel" next to the first point.

"Angels, created in His image by His design within His plan, even with free will, should not be capable of committing a sin worthy of such punishment without His knowledge long before their creation. But that's a topic for another day."

Luke's face flushes red as if he's about to argue, but he remains silent and leans back.

Seir places the chalk down and scans the class. "What are some prominent angels in Christianity?"

Lucille raises her hand, and Seir nods at her. "Archangel Gabriel—"

Before she can add any others, Mark on the other side of the class chimes in proudly. "Archangel Michael."

Of course, they'd forget to mention the one angel who had God's favor until the infamous rebellion.

"Archangel Samael"

Seir's gaze flicks to me, and shock flashes across his features before disappearing as quickly as it came.

"Interesting."

Someone giggles and whispers by the door as Seir points to them. "You. Get out."

Veronica puts her hands to her chest. "Me?! Why?"

"Get out of my class before I have you expelled."

Her eyes get so wide I'm half expecting them to bulge out of their sockets as she blubbers and gathers her things.

Isn't that a little harsh?

"Trust me."

I do.

"Then you would understand that it wasn't too harsh."

She pauses by the door and turns to look at him. "I'll be speaking to my father about this."

Seir's grin widens. "Go ahead. I'd love to discuss how his daughter plotted the attempted sexual assault and exploitation of another student."

My jaw drops, and I feel the blood drain from my face as she looks at me with tears in her eyes before hurrying out the door. I glance at Rae, whose face contorts with rage, but I shake my head subtly.

A few heads turn in my direction, and an odd wave of shame washes over me.

How did you know?

"Read through part two of the textbook, please. We will review on Wednesday."

He steps to the private office on the far side of the room. They're rarely used, mostly for keeping private documents, tests and exams from prying eyes, but my pulse skyrockets when he holds the door open and scans the class before his gaze lands on me.

"Ms. Sharpe. A word, please."

I stand, an odd mixture of nervousness and residual embarrassment coating my veins with each step toward the front of the room. I walk past his tall figure, and it's like my body has a visceral reaction to his. Regardless of what truth he just exposed, it's as if my mind acknowledges it, but with every inch I get closer to him, my heart wins the battle of emotions.

It's like my body craves to be close, but some small voice my mind is convinced that this has to do with Veronica.

The two emotions conflict and war with one another, vying for first place as I step into the mid-sized office and move to stand beside the large oak desk. There are various papers littered across it, but they look like they haven't been touched in months.

The door clicks shut behind me, and I turn to see Seir lock it before facing the center of the room. His piercing blue gaze pins me in place as he steps closer, until we're inches apart.

"Are you alright?"

Yeah, I mean I was shocked, but I'm not upset.

"Are you sure?"

Nodding, I wring my hands together.

Yes. Positive.

"Why do you still seem on edge?"

My heart pounds, and I can feel it in my throat.

I don't know how to put it into words without sounding crazy.

How do you tell someone of this kind of desire without objectifying them.

He takes a step closer and his hands glide to the sides of my neck, using his thumbs to tilt my head toward him.

Does it make me insane that I crave another kiss with an extra terrestrial?

He leans in with his dark hair falling forward and smiles against my lips as my heart rattles in my chest.

"I selfishly hope you never regain sanity, then."

His lips capture mine and at first, they're slow, lazy movements. Drawn out as if there isn't an entire class of people sitting in the other room. His kisses are savoring. Selfish, and greedy, with his fingers flexing into my hair at the back of my neck.

I could kiss him until the last day of my life.

He steps in closer, and the moment his chest crowds my space, one of his hands glides down to my collar, over my chest and along my stomach before he reaches down along my hip.

"We should stop."

His fingers glide down the back of my leg before he grips my thigh, hooking it around his waist.

We should.

Leaning me back against the desk, the edge of the wood bumps against my ass as he presses his hips into mine, swallowing the gasp with his mouth as the friction sends desire radiating through my body.

"I would die a million painful and torturous deaths if it meant hearing the sounds you make when I bring you pleasure."

The faint sound of chatter outside the room must give him more confidence, and he breaks our kiss to search my face. Whatever he sees there darkens his eyes, sending a shiver down my spine, and he leans in. His dark hair fills my vision as he presses his lips down the column of my throat to my collar while unbuttoning my blouse.

Kisses pepper my chest as my fingers intertwine with his hair, and his free hand squeezes my hip as he tugs my bra down. My mouth drops open as I watch the most handsome man I've seen in my life glance up at me with bright blue eyes before taking my nipple into his mouth.

He sucks hard, and my eyes roll back.

"That look you just made. That is my own eternal paradise."

He straightens and places another long, drawn-out kiss to my lips as chatter outside grows louder. When a loud thud echoes through the door, he pauses as he holds me close.

And all of a sudden, I understand why angels sinned.

He smiles against my lips, and my chest squeezes almost to the point of pain.

"Damn everyone who keeps me from you."

When he pulls back, I'm breathless, gripping his arm as he searches my face.

Seir.

"Yes, Oriana?"

Are you afraid at all of what is happening between us?

The question must take him off guard as his features turn contemplative before softening.

"I can count on one hand how many times I've been afraid in my life, Oriana. There is only one thing I fear, and this is not it."

I frown, and he releases my thigh, buttoning my blouse and leaning his forehead against mine.

What is it that you fear?

He hesitates, and for the first time, uncertainty flashes across his features. Before he can answer, someone shouts from the other room. With a sigh, he scans over me one last time, and his lips twitch.

"Well, you look a little flushed but otherwise the same as you did when you came in."

Extending his hand between us, I glance down at it as my heart thunders.

So you didn't actually need to have a word with me?

He laughs and my brow raises at him.

"I said a word... or two... didn't I?"

The sly look on his face sends butterflies through my body as he winks, placing his hand at the small of my back before leading me to the door.

Is it wrong of me to want to stay in here with you?

The moment the thought crosses my mind, I cringe internally at my own admission, chiding myself for the raw and unfiltered sentiment.

But his gaze just softens even more as his hand wraps around the door handle.

"I can't tell you how desperately I want you to always feel that way."

A sense of impending doom accompanies his words, and I frown, but before I can ask, he twists the handle. The door opens as everyone quiets down, and I cross my arms over my body as I pad to my seat.

Seir makes his way to the desk before sliding into his chair, and his piercing blue eyes scan the room. "Those who are done reading can go. See you all on Wednesday."

Rae scoots closer."What did he say to you?"

I shake my head, unable to verbalize what just happened, even if I wanted to. "Later, Rae."

My voice is barely a whisper, partly because I'm still trying to catch my breath and partly because I don't want my voice to betray my nerves.

As Rae leans back into her chair, I open my book, but my mind struggles to focus on the text. My eyes keep drifting to Seir at the front of the room.

Could there be something going on? Something I don't know about?

Uncertainty coats my veins like gasoline to the fire of anxiety burning in the back of my mind, and my imagination runs wild. First, I convince myself of the small inconveniences that could bring something between us, or cause him to leave. It's not until I consider what that that reality would be like, and I start to really feel the pit in my stomach grow.

That must be it. He's going to leave.

Why else would he have said that with such a tone?

My mind races with what his absence would bring, and the tight feeling in my chest only constricts more, so much more that it's nearly to the point of pain.

After a few moments, my heart skips a beat when I find him already looking at me.

"I'm not going to disappear on you, you know."

I swallow thick against the sudden clog of emotions in my throat as my eyes drop to the page again.

"Ori."

His words from earlier echo in my mind as my eyes lock with his. It's like he can see through to every vulnerability, every insecurity and deep-seated worry as my chest squeezes again.

"Oriana Sharpe listen to me very closely. There is not a single person in this world, nor on any other planet within this existence or in this universe that could keep you from me."

I blink, and tears well in the corner of my eyes.

Promise?

"I swear it on everything I am."

The fierce look in his eyes sends butterflies through my body, and I swallow.

"Ori," Rae whispers, "Do I need to beat the shit out of someone?"

I laugh quietly, shaking my head. "Not even close."

She blows out a breath of relief. "Well good. I didn't wanna get expelled."

People start shuffling around, and I glance at the clock to see that the hour is almost over. Dread settles in my chest as I pack my things into my bag. My attention flicks to Seir as I sling my bag over my shoulder, only to see his eyes already on me.

"Try to enjoy the rest of your day, Ori."

I nod, not caring if anyone is watching, and leave the class with Seir's gaze burning a hole in the back of my head.

Chapter 17

Over the next few hours, I feel like I'm in a daze. Part of me is day-dreaming about Seir, while the other part of me is frustrated, and trying to force myself to stay focused on my classes.

Leaving my last class of the day, Rae murmurs into her cell phone with her brows pulled together as she hangs up and shoves her phone into her pocket.

My gut twists, and I'm dreading asking, but I still do. "What's wrong?"

Her head snaps in my direction, and she chews her cheek nervously. "Merrick isn't pressing charges."

I frown. "Wasn't his wife hell bent on it?"

She nods, her gaze darting around before she answers, "Apparently, his wife got into a huge argument with your public defender. I guess there was some sort of evidence brought forth, and they basically legally blackmailed him."

I blink at her, completely dumbfounded. "So no charges?"

She grins from ear to ear. "None."

Elation coats my veins, and I'm about to inwardly tell Seir when someone bumps my shoulder roughly, causing me to stumble forward. Rae catches my arms as Veronica stomps past and out the front door, her head tilting slightly in my direction with a glare.

"I don't usually want to stab people," Rae whispers, "but her, I would easily get stabby with."

I blink at her, and we both laugh. "What's her problem anyways? I didn't even know anything about her until today."

Rae shrugs. "All I know is her dearest daddy is on the board of directors for the school and he's one of the biggest donors to DCC."

Divine Covenant Cathedral is the church my parents invested their lives into, and the reason I pulled myself from the church entirely. I saw how the church's influence changed them, turning them from loving parents into strict, righteous people demanding sacrifice from a child who was just trying to learn.

"Somehow I'm not surprised that Veronica's father is the biggest donor."

We descend the front steps as Veronica gets into a large white SUV. The driver looks like an official bodyguard hired by a mafia boss—black sunglasses, shaved head. The only thing missing is tattoos, but that wouldn't fit the bill for her family.

"You know, Ori," Rae starts, "we could have gone to community college."

My eyes slide to her, and we both burst out laughing. "Honestly, maybe we should have."

I can't bring myself to say it with conviction, though, because some part of me knows there's a chance I never would have met Seir.

"So what happened in the private office with Mr. Harvard? What did he want?"

Heat rises to my cheeks, and as she stares at me, I see her face blanch in my peripherals. Rae would never judge me, but I can't even process what happened without my body reacting in a way that's intensely inappropriate for a student and a professor.

"Substitute professor, actually."

I blink, pulling the cover over my mind.

Shit. I need to get better at doing that proactively.

"Ori, are you going to tell me or should I just assume that was the quickest quickie of the century?"

My head turns to her, and my eyes are as wide as saucers. "Not only would I never do that with that many people in the next room, I also hardly know him!"

Rae shrugs. "You don't have to know someone to bone them."

"Rae!"

The laugh that escapes her is purely maniacal. "Listen, it's obvious stuff is going on between you two. Or at least, it is to me. Just remember that I am your best friend, and thus, I require best friend tea. Specifically romantic tea."

I swallow, glancing behind us before keeping my eyes on the sidewalk ahead. "We... we just made out that's all."

Rae's excitement grows, and she huddles in close. "I knew it! Was it just, like, kissing or was there touching and feeling?"

"Why do I feel like you are living vicariously through me right now?"

She just laughs. "Because I am! Mr. Harvard is hot as hell. I bet you every girl and guy in that class either wants him or wants to be him."

The laugh that escapes me is more strangled than anything else, and I cough to clear my throat. Rae gives me this look like I know as much as she does that it's the truth, and I can't disagree, but I refuse to say it out loud.

"I mean, come on, Ori. The man's body is fucking delectable. You can't tell me you wouldn't wanna eat off it."

"Rae! Oh my gosh."

She just grins wider as we turn onto the last street, but her eyes narrow as she frowns. "Whose car is that?"

I follow her gaze to the black sedan down the road. Its windows are so darkly tinted that I'm nearly certain it's illegal, because not even the outline of the drivers or passenger side shows regardless of the sun shining on it. The neighbors three doors down tend to have family come in from out of town a few times a year, so I shrug, brushing it off.

"I have no idea. Maybe someone visiting next door?"

Her brows pinch together more, and she eyes it warily. "I dunno. Let's just get inside." Her eyes stay glued to the car as we cut down the pathway to our front door. The key unlocks with a click, and the door swings open before we pad inside and lock it behind us. Rae immediately walks to the window, and peers out at the car in the blinds.

"Relax, Rae. It's probably just the neighbors."

She says nothing as she watches, and it's a long minute before she peels her eyes off it, moving away from the window to take her shoes off.

"Nothing wrong with being nosey." She tosses her bag down by the door. "I was invited for dinner at Brad's house tonight, are you going to be okay by yourself?"

I put both hands on my hips. "Do you think I need a chaperone?"

She laughs and waves her hands between us. "No, no. I was just asking. I dunno. Forget it. I'm less worried about you now than I have been in months." Her eyes slide to mine, and a mischievous look dances across her features. "Besides, maybe this will give you an opportunity to invite Mr. Harvard over."

My mouth drops open, but before I can argue, she's already walking away, waving her hand in the air dismissively. "I'll be gone in an hour!"

Chapter 18

By the time she's coming down the stairs, dressed in a nice pair of jeans and a button-up blouse, nearly two hours have passed. Carrying a laundry basket of dirty clothes, I turn to look at her with a grin.

"Fashionably late?"

She shrugs. "He said take your time, so I did."

We share a look before laughing, and she shakes her head. "His parents were running late. Something to do with some meeting with the other board members."

"They're board members too?"

She nods, slipping on her one-inch heels. "Yeah, that's how I knew Veronica's dad was on the board for DCC. Brad's dad is on it too. Here, see—" She pulls out her phone and types something into her browser, before handing me a page that shows all six board members of DCC.

My stomach feels like a bag of rocks as I see Veronica's dad with the other five portraits. "Oh."

With both shoes on she levels me with a look. "They're not that bad, Ori. Sure, they say a lot of godly stuff, and like, they quote the bible, but they haven't been as strict as your parents were. I think they're okay."

I nod. "Sure. Well... I hope you have a good dinner."

Grabbing her purse, she stands and strides closer, hugging me from the side. I lean into her, unable to return the hug with my arms full of laundry.

"See ya later, Ori!" she calls out as she opens the door. I see a white sedan with its hazards on parked in front of the pathway. The door clicks shut behind her, and a moment later I hear it click as she locks the bolt.

I really need to get past this unease about the church.

She's right. Not all of them will be as strict as my parents. I should be giving benefit of the doubt until they prove otherwise.

If the law can do it, so can I, right?

Shoving the dirty clothes into the washer, I throw detergent in and turn it on before closing the door, hearing the water steadily pouring into the machine.

I mean, Seir was convinced his powers would make me go running, and I gave him the benefit of the doubt.

And look how that has been going.

Just because I have experience with parents within the church doesn't mean I should assume that every family is like that.

Thinking of what Seir said about his own family, I frown as I pace to my bedroom.

I wonder what drove him to do what he does today.

Reflecting on his approach with Vince, it makes me wonder whether he does this out of his own experiences too.

The look Seir gave me in his private office flashes into my mind, along with the feeling of his hand behind my thigh, and my body heats.

As my pulse hikes up, I replay each second in my mind—from the moment I walked past him in the doorway to him unbuttoning my blouse. By the time the memory is done, my chest rises and falls deeply with each breath.

Desire throbs in my body, demanding to be satiated, and the toy on my nightstand comes into my line of vision as I give it a lingering glance.

I guess it couldn't hurt.

My pulse quickens as I grab the soft silicone toy, finding the small power button on the side of the rose beside another button to change the mode.

The memory of Seir's hands on my body lingers in my mind as I lie down, not bothering to remove my skirt. Tugging my underwear off, I kick it aside with my stomach flipping as I press the power button.

A buzzing sound fills the room as the small hole starts to suck in air and I press the mode button, changing the rhythm to a stutter.

I file through each before turning it on low and slow.

Here goes nothing.

The anticipation sends desire pooling in my body. My pulse hikes even more, and I press it down onto my clit as the sensations send my mind into a whirl.

Oh, god.

I gasp and my eyes flutter closed as my legs twitch involuntarily.

My hips gyrate and I writhe as my breaths come in quick, and the way my body moves reminds me of being in the room with Seir. His hands on my body, the way it felt like he was restraining himself but still being greedy.

The way it felt like he needed to feel me sends another wave of desire lower in my body as little bolts of pleasure radiate from my clit.

The sudden feeling of being watched has my eyes flick open, and my gaze lands on Seir leaning against the wall. His dress shirt is unbuttoned halfway, the arms rolled up, and even from here I can see the bulge of his erection straining against his dress pants.

I'm about to pull the rose toy away as his voice echoes in the room amidst the buzzing. "Don't stop."

This has to be a dream.

A smile tugs at his lips. "If that makes you feel better, Ori," he teases as his piercing blue eyes scan my body. "Just don't stop."

"I—" My heart feels like it could explode at any second. "I've never... and to do this while being watched..."

He hesitates, searching my face. "Would you rather I leave?" The look on his face is genuine, and I shake my head.

"No." My voice comes out breathless. *That's the last thing I want. I just don't know how to ask for it without seeming...*

"Greedy?" He finishes my sentence for me, and I nod as he steps closer.

"Let me set the record straight, Oriana. Of the two of us, I am by far the greediest. Asking for something you want doesn't make you greedy. Taking it without permission does."

He steps up beside the bed, and I feel entirely exposed with a toy between my legs still humming and vibrating close to my clit, though thankfully the suction isn't in place.

His hands extend between us. "If I may?"

I blink at him, lifting the toy slightly. "This?"

The heat on his face blends in to his amusement as he nods as I pass it to him. My cheeks burn seeing the front of the toy wet as he turns it around and clicks the power off.

He watches me for a moment before glancing at it. "Have you ever tasted yourself, Ori?" I shake my head, and he raises his brow, "Do you want to?"

The look on his face is heated and dark as I nod in response. He pulls the top bedsheet off the bed and ties it around the post of the headboard tightly.

"What are you doing?"

He unbuckles his belt with one hand, and my heart rate jumps. "Giving you less to think about," pausing, he tilts his head. "Do you trust me?"

"Yes." I answer without hesitation, and emotion flickers across his face.

"Good. I won't hurt you, Oriana. Not now, not ever," he whispers, placing the toy on the side table, and leaning over my body with one knee between my thighs.

"Are we going to...." I trail off, and an odd mixture of disappointment and relief washes over me when he shakes his head.

I don't know that I'd be ready to go that far, even if everything in my mind is screaming to.

"No. But selfishly, I want to be a part of this." He looks down at me as his arm jerks to the side, and the belt tightens around my wrists.

Placing the toy on my stomach, hovering over me with his arms on each side of mine, his chest rises and falls beneath the opening of his shirt. His biceps flex as he leans onto his forearm, and the material constricts around his arms as I swallow nervously.

"If it's too much, just say stop and we will."

His knee between my legs, how close he is, the air he breathes skating over my skin.

God.

I'm more concerned about begging him not to stop.

His lips twitch. "If that's what you want, all you need to do is ask." He raises a brow thoughtfully. "Or demand."

"Seir," I whisper, "did you know what I was doing when you showed up?"

He leans in, holding his lips a hairsbreadth from mine. "No. You went silent, and I was worried."

My chest squeezes, emotion mixing with the desire growing in my body as he presses his lips to mine.

At first it's soft, tentative even.

Like the first taste of a dessert you want to savor.

But with each movement of his lips, his kisses get more urgent, and I lean into him, tugging against the gentle restraints.

Tasting him on my tongue is the most intoxicating thing I've experienced, and my system hasn't stopped craving him since that moment in his office.

His body weight leans down further, like he can't stop himself as my body reacts in tandem, my legs inching toward him.

Kissing down my neck to my chest he sits back slightly, taking the toy from my stomach and presses the power button. Buzzing fills the air as he pins one of my legs down.

My heart beats fast, and the moment he gently presses the mouth against my clit, my legs twitch against him, and I gasp. My hips gyrate against the sensations as my clit throbs, but no matter how much I move, he holds it in place.

"That's it, Ori. You're not leaving this room until you've come for me." His voice is thick as he watches me, keeping it in place despite my hips moving of their own volition.

He clicks the mode on the toy and the intensity increases as I squeeze my hands into fists over my head. My movement knocks the headboard around with a rhythmic thud and pleasure builds in my core.

My breathing is all that breaks the buzzing in the room, and my legs instinctively flex closed as he pins them in place.

At this point you could keep me like this for the rest of my life and I wouldn't care.

"A few hours of you beneath me like this might be too much for your mind to handle, Oriana."

He clicks the intensity up to the highest setting just as my mouth drops open to speak, and I whimper, "For you, I'd be able to handle it." I manage to get out between panted breaths.

He releases my legs and I wrap them around him instinctively before he leans in close. Easing pressure off my clit for a moment, I take in a deep breath.

"You'd take it all for me?" He whispers against my lips, pressing the rose against my clit, and I whimper.

"Yes."

"Even if it would make you a slut, a whore, a nympho?" He presses down further with the toy, and I gasp.

"Yes."

My orgasm is cresting just beneath the surface and with each ministration of the rose, I get closer and closer until I'm grinding my hips toward it.

Oh god, I'm so close.

"That's it, my filthy fucking slut needs to come." His lips crash against mine, and he grinds his body in time to the rhythm, mirroring my own movements as my orgasm shudders through me.

 My legs twitch, my body clamps down on nothing, and Seir captures my lips, breathing hard like he's the one who just came. He tosses the rose to the side of the bed and kisses his way down my chest.

What are you doing?

When he's between my legs, I'm still coming down from the waves of euphoria when his head dips below the pleats of my skirt.

"I told you, I'm greedy, Ori."

No sooner has he gotten my name out when his tongue glides up the length of my pussy. My eyes threaten to roll to the back of my head as he sucks and laves, squeezing my thighs that still twitch from my orgasm every time his nose and tongue hit my clit.

By the time he's crawling up my body, I'm utterly boneless, but desire still rages like a starved beast when he hovers over me.

With one hand he releases the belt restraint, and my arms fall limp for mere seconds before he presses his lips to mine again. Tasting the mix of my own arousal and him sends my mind into overdrive. My exhausted arms ease around his neck, and I don't miss the thick, throbbing erection beneath his dress pants as he leans his weight onto me.

Pausing he leans back, searching my eyes. "You are exquisite, Oriana Sharpe."

My heart swells, and he rolls onto the bed beside me before gathering me into his chest.

"I can't believe that just happened" I whisper, replaying everything in my mind as Seir's arms tighten around my body.

"It's a good thing I'm here to remind you that it did." His thumb glides along my hip and my foggy mind hones in on the movement.

I glance up at him, seeing him already lost in thought staring at the ceiling. "Do you always shield me from your thoughts or is your mind typically empty?"

His piercing blue eyes slide to mine. "I do try to keep most of my thoughts from projecting to you."

I frown. "Why?"

He's quiet for a long moment, and his fingers flex as I hear his heart rate hike under his chest.

"Do you not trust me?"

Shock flashes across his features. "Why wouldn't I?"

"Why else would you hide your thoughts?"

Seir releases a long sigh. "There are parts of my life you've yet to learn about, Ori. I can let you in more, if that helps, but there will be some things that must be kept private. Not because I want to, but because I must."

My brows pinch together more. "Why can't you tell me?"

There's a long moment of silence before he answers.

"Because it isn't safe, and I would fucking hate myself if you got hurt because of me."

I think if someone is going to risk their lives it should be up to the individual to decide if the risk is worth it.

"You don't understand, Ori. I wish I could explain, but even that is... It wouldn't matter if I didn't care so damn much."

My chest squeezes at his admission, and I nod against his chest.

Okay, we can make a deal. You keep yourself open to me more, but if you have to keep your secrets, I will trust you to do that.

His ocean blue eyes flick to mine before they flutter shut, and he leans in to place a kiss to my forehead.

"You've got yourself a deal, Oriana Sharpe."

Chapter 19

Hours later, I wake up to the sound of rain pattering against the window. Thunder rumbles in the distance, and I peel my eyes open to an empty bedroom. The sound of the front door closing sounds out, and I hear the click of heels for a couple paces as relief coats my veins.

Even if I have nothing concrete to be afraid of, because Seir hasn't shared anything specific with me, I still heard the unspoken message loud and clear that something could be dangerous for me.

Footsteps pad to my doorway as I sit up slightly, and Rae's head peers into the room. "Ori? You're awake."

I nod. "Yeah, just woke up not long ago because of the storm."

She walks in, wrinkling her nose in the dim moonlight. "Smells like sex in here." Her gaze flicks to the vacant nightstand, and she grins, "Ah, cause solo sexy time happened!"

My cheeks burn. "How was your night?"

She shrugs, and I just barely catch the movement from the flash of lightning illuminating the window. "Brad's family is fine. They have moments where they can be judgy, but overall they were nice. His dad apparently knew yours, he kept talking about how they used to be old golfing partners."

I frown. There isn't a time where I can remember my dad talking about golfing at all.

"Who is his dad?"

Rae moves to the window to crack it open. "Harold Godfrey."

Shaking my head, I ease my feet to the floor before plugging the rose toy in, and setting it on the nightstand. "I don't recognize the name at all."

She just shrugs again, walking to the door. "Oh well, maybe he was mistaken. He seemed sure, but who knows. I'm going to get some sleep though so I'm not a freaking zombie tomorrow."

"Okay, night Rae."

"Night Ori," She calls out from the hallway, with her footsteps growing more faint. As lightning illuminates the room, I move to close the door behind her before crawling into bed once again.

Mulling this over is a problem for tomorrow.

~

The next morning is relatively quiet. As we leave our third class of the day, I'm putting my books into my locker when I hear my name called from behind me.

"Ms. Sharpe." I turn to see Adam, the school's academic advisor, standing a few feet away. "Do you have a moment?"

Immediately, I start running through the reasons why he could be standing in front of me, but I come up empty. My grades are good so far, and I'm early into my first year, so it's not like I'm at risk of not having enough credits to graduate.

"Uh, sure."

He gestures down the hallway, and my heart leaps into my throat as I secure the bolt on my locker before stepping alongside him. He leads us to the administrative offices, and holds the door open to a room where a middle-aged man is seated.

The man stands quickly, smoothing his suit and giving us an awkward smile. "Ah, you must be Ms. Sharpe. It's good to meet you." He adjusts his glasses as we step closer before reaching his hand out between us. The moment my hand slides into his he gives it a tentative shake.

"I am." I say quietly. "I'm sorry, who are you?"

He flashes a grin that looks more like a grimace than anything. "My name is Harry Barclay, I'm a counselor employed by the school to assist with student evaluations."

My heart instantly drops.

Oh god, what if they know.

"I'm with you, don't worry."

His voice sounds oddly more concerned than expected, which only serves to heighten the anxiety gripping my chest.

I glance nervously between Adam and Harry. "Uh, it's good to meet you. What is this about?"

Adam moves to his desk and sits, gesturing to the empty seat beside Harry. "We'd like to offer an opportunity for you to get some on-the-job shadowing since your career aspirations are within this area."

Relief crashes over me, and I nod. "Yes, that would be great. Is it here at the school?"

Harry shakes his head before releasing a long sigh. "No, due to privacy restrictions, being involved in other student's counseling is prohibited. But, we do have a handful of individuals I work with who had graciously offered to be part of the shadowing program when they started seeing me."

Adam leans onto his forearms with his hands clasped together on the desk. "We can start as early as today. It will give you an extra credit if you manage to get 150 hours of on-the-job training for the year."

This feels too good to be true—an extra credit and training?

Still, deep down I know I'd be stupid to turn an opportunity like this away.

"Sure, that sounds good."

Adam's face lights up. "Great! Harry, when is the first—"

"Four-thirty. I believe that is right after your last class, correct, Ms. Sharpe?" Harry interrupts eagerly, his looks smile tense, and I nod. "Wonderful. I'll meet you outside near the parking lot then."

Adam stands and walks to the door, holding it open as I follow. "Well, it was lovely seeing you Ms. Sharpe. Hope you have a wonderful day."

"Uh, thanks so much."

By the time I'm in the hall, the door has already swung halfway closed behind me without so much as another word.

"Do you really need the extra credit?"

I tighten my grip on my bag, and start walking toward my last class of the day.

No, but it would be good to have just in case.

"Just in case? Are you anticipating failing?" The tone in his voice is of genuine concern, but I can't help feeling defensive in response.

It's my schooling, I should be allowed to make these decisions to give myself cushion. What does it matter if I'm not failing right now?

My brows pull together as a student brushes past me, and I turn the final corner.

I don't think anyone anticipates failing, but there's no harm in doing it to have the extra credit and experience. What is the problem, Seir?

There's a long pause before he responds, sounding as if he's restraining himself.

"Nothing."

I pull the cover over my mind and roll my eyes as I head to my desk.

I wonder what crawled up his ass.

Chapter 20

Class drags on, and though I'm tempted to lift the cover on my mind, I keep it in place.

I know that if I do fail any classes, it'll be because I wasn't paying enough attention, and Seir isn't going to help with that. We file out of the room, and I turn down the hallway toward the front as the hair on the back of my neck stands up.

"I vaguely remember being asked not to shut someone out recently," Seir's voice sounds out beside me, and my heart leaps into my throat.

"Well—" I begin to say, but the words get caught in my throat as my gaze snags on Merrick standing by the front door, speaking to none other than Adam and Harry. Outside of the bruising that has turned yellow, he looks surprisingly well healed before he turns away, walking out to the parking lot as my steps slow.

"Ori!" Rae's voice carries through the crowd as she hurries down the hallway, and I glance back where Seir was standing, only to find he's vanished.

I'm unsure whether I'm more relieved that Seir may have seen him, or anxious about Merrick's sudden presence.

"Ori, you good?" Rae says, tilting her head, "And where did Mr. Harvard go?"

"Uh, yeah. Adam came to get me today and said they have OJT for me." I glance down the hallway, seeing no sign of Seir. "He said he had to go."

Her eyes light up. "Oh. No way you got OJT set up! That's great. When do you start?"

Forcing a smile, I gesture to the front door where Harry stands. "Now. I have 37 hours per semester to complete. It'll be a lot to catch up on, but it should help."

"So, this means you're not walking home then, right?" She watches Harry and Adam before turning her gaze to me.

I shake my head. "No, I'm not even sure how late I'll be home."

She grasps my hand in hers. "Alright, well. I'm going to Brad's tonight for a bit, so, I might not be home when you get there."

"Okay," I say as she leans in for a hug, "Just be safe."

"I will! Try to have some fun, Ori!" She says as she turns away and walks out the front doors.

Here goes nothing.

Blowing out a breath, my heart pounds as I push out the doors, and take long strides until I'm standing before both men.

"Hey, sorry I'm late." My voice cracks, and I clear it as they look at me.

Adam's smile widens. "Ah, there she is! We were staring to wonder if you weren't going to show."

"Wouldn't dream of it"

Although I'm starting to.

Seir's laughter echoes in my head, and I'm about to cover my mind again when he suddenly speaks.

"Don't you dare cut me out, Oriana Sharpe."

His voice booms, the command in it has an edge that sends a shrill note of adrenaline through my veins as Adam and Harry glance over my shoulder and wave at someone.

Why?

"Well, we better get going. My car is just down the steps." Harry says, and Adam waves before turning toward the school. A lump forms in my throat, but I follow Harry as he descends the stairs.

"Because I need to be sure you're okay."

I'm with someone from school, I'll be fine.

"Liam was from your school, too."

Point taken.

By the time we reach the car, my palms are clammy, and my pulse rages in my ears.

It'll be fine.

We'll just drive down the street and everything will be A-OK.

The car beeps as it unlocks, and Harry climbs into the driver's seat. I exhale shakily, sliding into the passenger side and fastening my seatbelt.

If I die, Seir.... Just... get rid of the rose before they search my stuff okay?

His voice comes through strained.

"Fuck that. The rose stays, and nothing will happen to you."

Why do I feel like you like it more than I do?

"I already told you, I'm the greediest asshole you know, Ori."

My cheeks heat as Harry turns the wheel and drives out of the parking lot. We turn onto a main road, and he accelerates toward the highway.

"So, where are we going?" I ask, cringing when my voice wavers nervously.

Harry cuts in front of someone as they lay on their horn. "We're making a housc-call to an older patient of mine."

I nod, as if he can see me with his eyes on the road ahead. "Right. And he's okay with other people showing up?"

"Yeah. He signed an agreement saying we could use his sessions for shadowing through the college. He gets a well-discounted rate by doing it."

Harry swerves into another lane, quickly braking to turn onto another road, and my chest squeezes painfully.

I may die of a heart attack before anything actually happens to this vehicle.

"Don't do that, or I'll kill him."

My lips twitch, and the traffic light ahead turns red. The vehicle continues toward the intersection and with each passing second that he doesn't slow down, my heart stutters.

"It's red—" I hardly get the words out when Harry curses, slamming on his brakes as the car skids to a stop, and we both lurch forward into our seatbelts, but an invisible, gentle pressure keeps me from jerking too hard toward the dashboard.

Holy fuck.

"Correction. I may kill him regardless."

"Sorry about that," Harry says, adjusting his glasses. "I was lost in my thoughts for a moment and didn't notice. No harm done, right?"

I manage an awkward smile before focusing on the road again.

I might just help you.

Seir's genuine laughter rings out, and I have to bite back a smile.

I'm white-knuckling the seat by the time we reach a small residential neighborhood, and as we pull up in front of a small, well-kept house, I've never been happier for a vehicle to come to a stop.

Even your driving didn't give me this much anxiety, and you were driving like a maniac.

"That's because unlike with him, you're safe with me."

I swallow hard, getting out of the car as Harry does the same.

"So, I'll do most of the talking," Harry says, "but if you'd like to introduce yourself, feel free."

"Uh, sure."

I follow Harry up the front steps and ring the doorbell. After a long minute, shuffling sounds come from inside, followed by the bolt clicking and the door creaking open just enough to reveal an eye peering through.

"Harry is that you?" The old man squints at him as Harry laughs.

"You bet it is! Brought one of the students with me as well if you don't mind. Ms. Sharpe, this is Richard."

"Oriana. Pleased to meet you," I say, offering my hand between us.

Richard glances at my hand before shaking it. "Oriana. Beautiful name."

"Ah, thank you," I say quietly as he releases my hand and retreats into the house.

Harry holds the door open as we step inside. There's a musty odor that permeates the air, like the windows haven't been opened in months, but someone's lived their entire life in a single room.

Honestly with the size of the house, my assumption might not be far off. The house is hardly bigger than Rae's front room and kitchen combined.

Harry takes off his shoes, and I follow suit, staying somewhat close as he walks to the living area. Richard sits on a rocking chair in the middle of the room facing the television as Harry sits closest to him along the couch.

I sit down a few inches away at the opposite end from Harry as Richard drapes a blanket over himself.

Harry clicks his pen and hovers the tip over his notepad. "Well, how have things been since we last talked?"

Richard shrugs. "About the same. Hearing things a little worse than before."

Harry nods, scribbling something down. "Is anything going better?"

There's a long moment of contemplative silence before Richard sighs. "I finally made it to bingo the other night."

"Well that's great!" Harry says, sitting up straighter. "You've been wanting to do that for a while. How did it feel?"

Richard grimaces. "Well I got there, saw people standing by the doors and left."

Harry puts his finger up, wagging it back and forth. "Ah, but you still went, and that counts."

My gaze shifts to the window as the sun disappears behind a cloud, darkening the room.

Richard waves his hand dismissively. "I'm too old for participation points," he grunts, flicking the television off before tossing the remote down.

"Mind if I use your restroom, Richard?" Harry asks, standing up and stretching.

"Have at it, my new friend Oriana will keep me company."

Harry disappears around the corner as Richard waves me over. "Come here and let me get a better look at you."

Unease settles in my stomach, but I stand up, smoothing the pleats of my skirt before stepping nearer. When I'm within reach, he grabs my hand, and I gasp as he pulls me in close.

His eyes are wild as he searches my face. "You. You've been marked by the devil. They can't see it but I do. I see it, I hear it. You're marked for death by demons."

My heart rages as his grip tightens. "Ah, you're hurting me." I whisper, and he abruptly releases me as Harry comes around the corner again.

"Alright, now that that's—" Harry's voice cuts off as he glances between us. "Is there a problem?"

Swallowing hard, I shake my head. "Nope. None at all."

Seir...

"Oriana was just telling me about how well her classes were going." Richard says, giving Harry a grin as he sits back down on the couch.

Harry's eyes dart back and forth between us. "Oh, I see. Yes, she's a rather well-performing student with an affinity for counselling herself."

Seir.

At this point my desperation to hear his voice is paramount, and I sit down on the couch in a daze, zoning out as Harry resumes his line of questions for Richard.

When the hour is up, I nearly sprint from the house, barely managing a goodbye to Richard, and relief washes over me when I see Seir's car parked next to Harry's.

Oh, thank God.

"I'll drop you off at home, what is your add—" Harry starts to say as I cut him off abruptly.

"Oh, that's my ride. Thank you, Harry!" I hardly get the words out when Seir gets out of the driver's side, walking around to the passenger door before holding it open.

Isn't it bad for me to be seen with my substitute professor?

Seir's eyes are still fixed on Harry, and if I didn't know any better, I'd say he was murdering him in his mind repeatedly. My lips twitch, and when I reach the door, his gaze slides to me.

"Are you okay?" His ocean blue eyes search mine, and I nod.

"I am now," I whisper, sliding into the seat as he closes the door and watches Harry get into his car. Seconds later, Harry's tires screech as he accelerates out of the neighborhood, and I can't help but blow out a breath of relief.

Seir climbs into the driver's side, opens the door, and settles behind the wheel.

"What the hell was that?" My voice is hardly a whisper as I glance over at Seir.

He studies my face for a moment. "Why did you cut me out again?"

My heart drops as I run through every moment from leaving Harry's car to stepping out of the house. "I didn't. I called out to you twice after... You didn't hear me?"

The flash of emotion on his face could only be described as panic as he shakes his head. "No. When you stopped responding I tracked down Harry's car, and came straight here."

I blink at him. "You did all of that because I—"

He tilts his head and leans in close. "Oriana, you told me you weren't going to cut me out. So, when you did, I assumed something was wrong."

I swallow thick against the emotions clogging my throat.

So you really don't hear me?

His expression shows no indication of hearing my thoughts as I frown. "So you really didn't hear me two seconds ago?"

He shakes his head. "No, and what's worse is that I don't know why."

A heavy dread settles in my stomach like a sack of rocks. "Why am I so scared that you can't?" I whisper, and Seir's gaze softens as he presses the button to turn the car on before putting it into drive.

He intertwines our fingers, pulling my hand into his lap and rubbing his thumb soothingly along my skin. "Everything will be okay, Ori."

I squeeze his hand slightly and chew the inside of my lip as he merges onto the main road. He accelerates hard, like he's trying to race the clock as he speeds onto the ramp to the highway.

Even though he's speeding, and maneuvering between other lanes filled with vehicles, somehow I feel less concerned about that than Harry's driving earlier.

No, the only thing I'm terrified of right now is why we suddenly can't hear one another.

"What does this mean, Seir?" I ask softly, and his attention flicks to me as the descending sun shines through the front windshield.

"I suspect it has to do with the spell Rae cast the night I first heard you."

"Do you think the spell wore off?"

Seir's grip tightens on my hand. "I don't know."

Part of me thinks I should tell him what Richard said, but another part of me just wants to brush it off or forget it happened. I'm conflicted as we turn onto the familiar sight of Rae's street.

When police lights and smoke billowing into the air catch my eye, my mouth drops open in shock. "Oh my god."

Firetrucks line up outside the house, spraying water into the building as I frantically search the crowd for any sign of Rae as we pull up closer.

"Ori, you need to be careful."

"What if Rae was in there?" My voice is shrill, and I look around wildly before turning to Seir.

He looks calm, but on high alert as he pulls over and puts the car into park. I'm about to unbuckle my seatbelt when he reaches over, halting my movements with his hand on my arm.

"Ori, listen to me. I'm sure Rae is fine, but you need to be careful."

Be careful?

My best friend could be dead!

"I need to find her." I whisper, wrenching my arm from his grasp and bolting from the car in one quick movement, ignoring him calling out my name. The smell of smoke stings my eyes as I scan the faces gathered along the street and head toward the firetrucks.

"Rae!" I shout, feeling Seir at my back before I sprint toward the firemen.

"Excuse me!" One of the firemen turn to face me as I cough through the smoke. "I live here. What happened?"

The fireman shakes his head. "We got a call that there was a house fire from one of the neighbors. We've managed to put out the active flame, but it looks like most of the place has been destroyed."

He grimaces, and I wrap my arms around my waist. "There's another person who lives here... was there anyone...?" I trail off, unable to finish my sentence as he shakes his head again.

"We didn't find any bodies inside yet, just destroyed property that we've seen."

My heart thunders as I turn to Seir. "Can I use your phone?"

He unlocks it and hands it over without a second thought. My hands fumble with the buttons as I dial her number, having to erase and redial it multiple times before I get it right.

The repetitive ringing sounds out in my ear until finally she picks up.

"Hello?"

"Rae!" Relief coats my veins like a balm to my soul, and my knees threaten to give out as Seir's arm wraps around my waist.

"Ori? What's going on? Whose number is this?"

"Rae, the house—it's gone."

There's a pause on the other end, and I hear a door close before Rae's voice comes through again. "What do you mean?"

"I mean I got back from OJT and there's firetrucks everywhere. The house is gone."

"Oh my god." She whispers. "You're okay though, right?"

I nod, even though she can't see me. "Yeah, I'm okay."

"I'll have to call my parents. I'll call you back."

The line clicks quiet, and I slide the phone from my ear to hold it against my chest before blowing out a breath.

Fuck. What do we do now?

Seir's grip on my waist loosens, and my eyes slide to him as he turns me around. "What did she say?"

I still feel like I'm in a daze. "She's going to call her parents. She'll probably see if she can use their spare bedroom now."

There's a tight feeling in my chest as I glance at the smoke billowing from the building. Movement in the crowd catches my eye, and I see someone in a hood turning and walking away.

"Alright, well, there's nothing we can do about this now." Seir says, intertwining our hands and guiding me toward his car.

"Where are we going?" I whisper as he opens the passenger door.

He cups my cheeks, and tilts my head up to meet his gaze. "We're going to my place to get dinner. If you end up wanting to stay somewhere else, I'll drive you."

My heart leaps into my throat, and I shake my head. "I can't ask that of you."

The smile he flashes in my direction as I slide into the passenger seat sends my mind into overdrive, and he leans in slightly.

"It's a good thing you're not asking then."

Chapter 21

My chest tightens as Seir closes the door, and I watch him walk around the front of the car.

Without having this mental connection, it's like I'm more focused on how he moves—the way he surveys the area with a seriousness that is such a stark contrast to the joyful, and lighthearted nature I'm used to seeing.

He moves with a graceful, almost stoic precision, but there's a calculating edge in his stride that reminds me of his dangerous side.

The guy nearly killed Merrick for god's sake.

He slides into the driver's seat and glances at me with a twitch of his lips. "Should I be concerned that you're staring at me like that?"

I blink. "Uh, like what?"

A smile graces his features as he puts the car into drive. "Like you're about to challenge my title as the greediest person we know."

My cheeks burn at the fact that he noticed, and he maneuvers the car between observers.

"I don't know what you're talking about."

He laughs, turning onto the main road as he steers with one hand. His other rests comfortably on the gearshift, and my eyes trace the veins along his hand. His fingers curl around it slightly, and my pulse rages as my gaze flicks to the road in front of us.

How the hell is even just his hand attractive to me?

The memory of calling his body beautiful flashes through my mind, making my cheeks burn hotter.

I guess maybe it's a small victory that he can't hear my thoughts right now.

The reminder is more bitter than sweet, and I frown. "Do you think the fire is the reason we can't hear one another anymore?"

His knuckles whiten, and his jaw feathers as he pulls onto a secluded road. "Unless you carry whatever you and Rae used to bind the two of us with you everywhere you go, I'm assuming the fire destroyed it."

My eyes widen. "The jar..."

He pulls into a driveway, and I see security personnel in the booth at the entrance. They grin at him with a nod of respect as he pulls past them before continuing inward.

He needs security?

"Where was the jar kept after you two cast the spell?"

I'm still confused, with my brows pulled together as a large house comes into view off to the side of us.

"In Rae's closet—" Another set of guards passes us before we turn into the actual driveway. "Is this your property?"

He laughs with a shrug. "It's safe, and nearby to most areas of the city without being too far." Pulling alongside the house, he cuts the engine and leans back.

"How far of a walk is it to the school, again?" I ask, raising an eyebrow as he laughs. It's so genuine that I find myself smiling with him as he collects himself.

"There's no way in hell you're walking to school. Especially not after tonight."

"What do you mean?"

There's a long pause, and the look on his face tells me he's choosing his words carefully, which only serves to heighten the anxiety rising in my chest.

"You don't think the fire was just an accident?"

His eyes meet mine, and the concern in them is clear enough that he doesn't need to answer.

"I think that it's an odd coincidence that you suddenly get job shadowing the same night that your home catches fire. Regardless of the impact to our connection."

Richards words echo in my mind, and I wring my hands nervously. Seeing Merrick today should have been warning enough.

"Oh god." I whisper, and Seir's head tilts as he searches my face.

"What is it?"

"Could it have been Merrick?" I ask, my voice hardly audible as my pulse rages in my ears.

"Hey," Seir cups my cheek, and my attention hones in on his touch. "Merrick won't be able to do anything to hurt you. Not while I'm with you."

The look he's giving me tells me he means what he's saying, but all it does is raise more questions.

Why does he care?

Why is he so adamant in helping me?

How can someone like him be interested in someone like me?

His brows pinch together like he's trying to read my mind. "Ori, say something."

I swallow thick against the influx of questions. "Why me?"

The question is double-edged, because on one hand, I don't know why Merrick would want to hurt me this badly when I don't even know what he was doing in his house. On the other hand, I don't understand why Seir would still be so willing to help me after our connection was broken.

He found me at Richard's, he showed up that night when I cut him out, he saved me at that party, and now he's helping me by letting me stay with him.

"There's a lot you have yet to learn about me, and this world we live in, Ori. I can't give you all the answers, but I can tell you arguably the most important one."

He leans in, bringing his face mere inches from mine as his gaze drops to my mouth.

"It might be hard to understand my reasoning when you hold yourself in lower regard than you should, but allow me to inform you that it didn't take long after meeting you to know you were special."

He's so close, that I don't dare breathe. My lungs freeze, my heart pounds, and his ocean blue eyes pin me in place as he continues.

"The moment you walked into that classroom, I knew I wanted you. When you were drunk at that party, I didn't give a fuck what the repercussions were, but I was going to get you out. It drove me mad to know that he had touched you, that he had you vulnerable, and I wasn't there to stop it. And the night I showed up to see you in bed, writhing, and panting as you pleasured yourself? I thought I'd lose my mind then and there. The only thing keeping me sane is knowing you're nearby—that in some way, I hold a small piece of you through the connection we have."

His thumb glides along my cheek as he pauses, and I manage a hardly audible whisper. "And now that the connection is gone?"

He gently presses his lips to mine, and my body comes alive for the briefest moment before he pulls back, keeping our lips a hairsbreadth apart.

"And now that the connection is gone, I find myself losing control. I have a knack for finding things, Ori, and it took me minutes too long to find you with Harry. I need you around me. To know you're safe, healthy and happy."

He crushes his lips to mine, and my mind goes blank as heat envelops my entire being. Fingers flexing against my skin, he slides his hand around the back of my head, curling his fingers into my hair.

By the time we pull apart, we're both breathing heavily, and desire coats my veins like hot oil.

I've never wanted someone like this before.

Seeing him is enough to send my mind into a haze, but the moment I taste him on my tongue, feel his skin against mine—I can't get enough.

"We should go inside," he whispers against my lips.

"We should," I agree, before closing the distance between us again, and he groans.

The sound sends desire straight to my core as he nips at my lip, and I gasp at the pain before he unclips my seatbelt. My body moves on autopilot and the material slides away from my chest before Seir uses both his hands to tug me over the center console.

Our lips hardly break apart as I climb over, straddling his waist as he eases the seat back slightly.

It gives me more space for my legs, but I couldn't care less at this point. Desire is a living, breathing creature in my body, and the only name on its lips is Seir's as a throbbing pulsates deep in my core. My clit craves pressure so badly that it aches, and as Seir's hand squeezes the back of my thigh, I press myself further into him.

He groans again, breaking our kiss for a brief moment, "You may be the death of me, Oriana Sharpe." He grinds into me, and the moment he does, the length of his dick beneath his pants squeezes my clit. I whimper into his mouth as he repeats the action, and my hips grind harder into him.

Oh, god it feels so fucking good.

I need more.

Fuck. I need him.

Pleasure continues to build in my core, and I pause, my entire body protesting as I pull back. "Seir—"

"Remember what I said about greed, Ori?" He's panting, his face is flush as he shoves the car door open.

"Yes," I breathe, "I remember."

He climbs out of the car with his arm hooked around my waist as I cling to him, and he slams the door shut with his foot, carrying me to the front door in quick strides.

"I'm about to remind you the difference between desire and greed, and maybe then you'll understand how greedy I can be when it comes to you."

Chapter 22

He hardly gets the last word out before he presses me against the door roughly.

With my back pinned to the hard surface, he crushes his lips to mine once more. His free hand pushes buttons on a pin pad until a beep chimes out, and within seconds I'm suspended in his arms again. The door behind me swings open with a creak, but I'm hardly paying attention as I lose myself in him.

He carries me up a set of stairs, down a hallway and into a room before kicking off his shoes and setting me down on a soft surface.

A bed.

Holy fuck.

Am I ready for this?

Looking at Seir as he pulls my shoes off, there's no doubt in my mind that I want him more than I've ever wanted anyone or anything in my life.

If I took all the desire, need and want in my life and concentrated it into one, it still would pale in comparison to what I feel for this man before me.

He leans in, his dark hair brushing my skin as he places kisses up my leg. "Last chance to change your mind, Ori."

His lips trail higher, his hands slide under my ass, and he hooks his fingers under the waistline of my skirt and underwear as his ocean blue eyes meet mine.

I shake my head. "I'm not going to change my mind."

His eyes flash with emotion, and he tugs my skirt down, pulling the material down my legs before tossing it aside.

My heart thunders as he unbuttons my blouse, easing it off both my arms before dropping it behind us. I go to unclasp my bra but his fingers curl around my arms, halting my movements as he searches my face.

Seir says nothing as his hands glide along my forearms before finding the hooks at my back. Ocean blue eyes once again suck me into their vortex as the material suddenly comes loose, and he pulls both straps off one at a time.

His actions are intensely intimate, and by the time my clothes are fully off, desire in my body rages like a wildfire. My fingers automatically move to his dress shirt, and I fumble but manage to get his shirt completely unbuttoned, helping him with the sleeves before he tosses it to the ground.

My hands are on his belt within seconds, and anticipation, nervousness, and desire are all vying for superiority as I tug it off before moving to his button and zipper.

My heart's in my throat as I pull his dress pants down with the waistband of his boxers, and the length of his dick springs free. It bobs between us, and I swallow.

Is it supposed to be this big? I've watched adult films before, but it's different when it's right in front of you and not on a screen.

I swallow, glancing up at Seir who has amusement painted on his features.

"Still not changing your mind?"

Holding his gaze, my fingers graze the skin along his thigh, and I don't miss the shiver or the goosebumps that break out before I finally reach his dick. Heat flashes across his face as my hand wraps around the length of his cock and glide up and down the length.

"Not a chance, Seir."

His eyes threaten to roll back with a flutter, and every part of me revels in the look on his face. He pulses in my hand, as if he could get any more hard than he already is, and his heated gaze settles on me once more.

Seir leans forward, and I release my grip on his dick as he wraps his hands under my thighs, kneeling on the bed as he lifts me into the air with surprising ease.

A shrill sound escapes me as he tosses me gently into the center of the bed before crawling on top of me, pressing light kisses along my neck before pausing to search my face.

"I find myself torn, Oriana." He presses his body onto mine, with his hard length squeezed between the weight of our pelvic bones as he leans in to kiss me once more.

A long moment passes and I pull back. "Why?"

"Because every part of me wants to fuck you, and use your body for my pleasure alone until I fill you to the brim with come. But there is also nothing more that I want than to feel you clench around me as you lose control of your body over and over until you no longer know your own name."

My breath hitches, and the way his eyes flash tells me he knows the way my body reacted to his words.

"But you'd like that wouldn't you?" he whispers against my lips, "My filthy fucking slut, the one who came undone for me mere nights ago." I hook my legs around his thighs as he grinds himself against my clit, as if to emphasize my need with pleasure.

Little bolts of euphoria sends more desire into my body, and I gasp against him, "Seir. Oh my god, please. I need more."

He groans, "Fuck, I will never get used to the sound of my name on your lips." His hand slides between us, and his thumb circles my clit as he eases a finger inside of me.

The feeling is foreign, but not unwelcome as he continues to circle, but everything inside of me wants all of him right now.

Fuck if there's pain.

I can't go another second....

"Seir, please."

His dick pulses against my leg, and he slides another finger in, the muscle in his jaw feathering as if he's doing everything he can to restrain himself.

"Beg me again, and I won't stop."

"Seir," He freezes, the look on his face pure warning, "Please, for the love of God, fuck me."

The low sound that escapes him as he withdraws sends a note of excitement down my spine. He wraps one arm around my waist, with the other hooking around the back of my neck as he kisses me deeply.

The way he kisses me is a language of its own as the head of his dick presses against my soaking wet pussy, and while my mind can't comprehend the words, my body sings. He pushes the tip in, and sharp pain suddenly shoots into my pelvic area as I whimper into his mouth.

"Damnit, Ori," He says against my lips, pausing as I catch my breath, "Do you have any idea what you do to me?"

He withdraws almost imperceptibly before pushing in again, and I breathe through the pain, digging my nails into his skin on instinct as I wince.

I just want the band-aid ripped off.

His movements are painfully slow, and I'm half thankful but also have frustrated because I need him, and I need him now.

He gets halfway in and pauses, letting me get another breather as I dig my heels into him, pausing as his hand wraps around my neck, and he looks into my eyes.

Whatever he sees has him adjusting his grip, "Just remember, you wanted this, Oriana."

His arm flexes around my waist, and he pushes deeper, the pain from his size even with how wet I am makes me cry out, but he doesn't stop until he's fully seated. By the time his balls lie flush to my ass, tears stain my cheeks, and we're both breathing each other's air.

"Seir?"

His ocean blue eyes are more piercing, and brighter than they've ever been as he searches my face.

"Remember how you said you'd never hurt me?" His eyes flash, but he nods as I continue, "I want you to forget that, because this kind of pain, I do not mind at all."

He chuckles, withdrawing halfway before leaning down to whisper in my ear, "Don't get me wrong, Ori. I'm very much a fan of pain mixed with pleasure, and you will experience it all, but I already told you I am the greediest person you know. I'm not about to make your first experience filled with pain, because I selfishly want more than that for you. For us."

My chest tightens, and he leans his head against mine, "Do you understand?" I nod, and his hair feathers against my forehead. Whatever existed between us, did not diminish at all when our connection broke.

My heart thunders as he presses his lips to mine, and pushes in deep with a deep groan. His hand glides up my thigh, his fingers flex against my skin.

By the time he's fully buried inside of me again, my entire body feels like I'm on the edge of an orgasm, and we've hardly gotten started.

There's no way I could be this close.

Could I?

He withdraws again slowly before driving in with more force than before, but there's no pain at all, and I dig my fingers into his back as my hips gyrate to meet his.

Seir breaks our kiss as he thrusts in again, leaning back get a better angle. He must know I'm close as heat flashes across his face, and he keeps his momentum as he drives into me.

"That's it, Ori. You're doing so fucking well."

My orgasm builds, and my entire body feels like it's become an inferno as my heart thunders.

"Seir, oh my god."

"Let go, Oriana." The command to his voice is clear, but it's thick with the same goddamned need I feel echoed in the very being of my soul.

He continues to drive into me, squeezing my clit with each thrust as he reaches depths of my body I didn't think was possible.

The euphoric feeling in my body heightens, builds and as he crushes his lips against mine again, it shudders through me. My limbs tense as he drives in deep and presses his weight down, moving his hips in time with mine as I clamp down on him.

I'm still riding each wave of pleasure as he squeezes me against his body, and pulsates deep as he comes. We're both breathing hard as he looks at me with a mixture of bewilderment, and something else I can't quite place.

"What are you thinking?" My voice is no more than a whisper, and my chest tightens as he leans down, pressing his forehead over my heart before placing a tender kiss against my skin.

"I'm thinking things that would probably terrify you," he whispers against my skin as he withdraws, shifting to lay alongside me. His hand wraps around my leg, tugging me into his arms, and gathering me against his chest.

"Are you going to murder me?"

The laugh that escapes him so suddenly is entirely unexpected, and I chuckle with him as he collects himself, shaking his head.

"I doubt it would scare me, especially if you're not going to murder me."

His arms tighten around my body. "I wish that were true."

I frown, tilting my head to look at him, and surprise rifles through me when he looks genuinely worried.

"Hey," I whisper, sitting up more to look at him. "Seir, tell me the truth."

His piercing blue eyes slide to mine, and I can see the weight of whatever he's hiding behind them. "I've always told you the truth, Oriana. Always have, and always will."

"So tell me what is weighing on your mind."

His mouth drops open as if he's going to finally tell me when his phone vibrates on the ground.

"I think that might be your friend." He whispers, and I blink before scrambling off the bed to snag his phone from the ground. Gravity works as both our releases start to slowly ease down my inner thighs.

I spot Rae's number on the caller ID and swipe to answer, "Hello?"

"Ori! Sorry, my parents have been on the phone with the fire department. It's been an entire ordeal."

I climb back into bed alongside Seir, and his arms encircle my shoulders once more, almost instinctively as he holds me close. With my head pressed against his chest, his steady heartbeat thumps in one ear as I keep the phone pressed to my other.

"That's alright. Are you at their place now?" Seir's fingertips trace along my side to my hip, and the lazy circles he makes with them threatens to distract me from Rae.

"Yeah, Brad dropped me off a few minutes ago while I was waiting for them to call back. Do you want to come sleep on the couch?"

I glance up at Seir, still uncertain somehow that he wants me to stay here, but the look on his face reassures me as I swallow.

"Uh, I've actually got a place to stay for now."

A choking sound sounds out before she makes a shrill cry, "Mr. Harvard?!"

Seir's lips twitch, and he mouths, "That fucking name," as I suppress laughter myself.

"Okay, well, I'll see you at class tomorrow then." She groans, and I just laugh.

"I'll see you tomorrow, Rae."

She grumbles a goodbye under her breath, and I click the end call button before handing the phone to Seir. My eyes track the movement as he places it on the other side of the bed, and his thumb glides soothingly along my skin.

He rolls me onto my back, lazily placing kisses along my collarbone and down my chest. When he reaches my breast, he glances up, holding my gaze as he takes my nipple into his mouth.

My back arches at the contact, and he sucks hard before moving to the next one. Desire begins to pool in my core again, and when he hovers over me again, I don't miss the way he throbs between us.

"Do you think you can take more, Ori?" He whispers, the tip of his cock pressed firmly against my entrance that's still dripping both our releases.

Seir presses his lips to mine again as I nod, and he exhales sharp as he pushes in again. The pain resurfaces as my body works to accommodate his size, and I whimper against his lips.

"I need you to tell me if you need to stop, but just know I'm going to push you further."

He eases himself deep in one long, steady motion as I breathe through the pain. "You're doing so well, Ori," he reaches over, tugging my left knee higher until it's hooked over his shoulder.

The angle only serves to deepen his reach, and I'm certain that if he pushed on my stomach he'd feel himself. The thought only sends desire pooling in my core, and I'm not ready when he withdraws halfway only to thrust inside hard.

I cry out, gripping the sheets as he wraps his hand around my neck, bringing my attention to him as he repeats the action.

"That's it. Eyes on me."

Each long, drawn out thrust feels ten times more intimate as he watches my reaction, and I fight the urge to let my eyes roll back. Each bolt of pleasure radiating from my clit threatens to send me overboard as another orgasm crests.

"One more, Oriana. Can you give me one more?" His tempo has picked up, and the urgency of it matches my own desperation as my hips move in time with his thrusts.

His grip on my neck tightens, and I'm lightheaded as my euphoria takes over my body. My legs twitch as my hips roll, squeezing down on him as he groans.

"That's it. You're so fucking perfect when you come for me." He pistons into me harder than ever before, like he can force himself impossibly deeper as the pressure builds in my stomach from the way he rearranges my organs. He releases his grip on my neck and pushes to his knees, keeping me suspended with one arm around my hips.

My body's still oversensitive from my orgasm, and the way he's driving into my body is borderline animalistic. It's nearly too much to handle, and I'm about to tell him to pause when he thrusts in deep, holding me in place as he comes.

Seir's breathing hard as he gathers me into his chest before easing onto his back, with his hands guiding us the whole way until I'm straddling his hips.

He's still fully seated, and I feel fully out of my element as he watches me with a half-lidded gaze. My legs feel like I've run a mile from how long they've been trembling, and beads of sweat trail down my chest as he reaches up to cup my breast.

"You're exquisite, Oriana Sharpe."

My eyes flick to his as he teases my nipple, and I feel him throb inside me as a heated look graces his handsome features.

I may not survive a full night with him.

He throbs again, and his free hand moves between my legs to circle my clit. The pleasure that jolts through my core at the contact is borderline painful with overstimulation, but desire pools in my core nonetheless as he does slow circles.

His piercing blue gaze searches my face, and he throbs again, and again until I feel him fully hard inside me.

"Can you give me one more?" he murmurs, withdrawing his hand from my clit to place both on my hips as he guides my movements. "Just like that. Ride my dick, just like that."

My hips rock back and forth as he continues to pulse inside me, and I'm certain I have lost my mind as he somehow feels even deeper than ever.

It's almost too much, but he continues to pull my hips forward and back with a hunger on his face that sends a thrill to my very being.

As if unable to help himself, he thrusts into my movements, "Do you feel what you do to me?" My orgasm crests as pleasure builds in my core, and he searches my face, "That's it, Ori. That's the spot, right there. Come for me."

My hips roll as I chase my pleasure that feels so close to exploding from my body, and he seems to know as my breathing picks up.

"Oh, God. Oh, fuck, I can't—"

Whether due to the position, or overstimulation, my orgasm crashes over me, my vision goes white, and my body clamps down hard as I dig my fingers into Seir's skin.

The sounds that escape my throat are uncontrollable as I ride out each wave of euphoria, and Seir's hand gently wraps around the base of my neck as he pulls me into him, and crashes his lips to mine.

"You did so well," he says between peppered kisses, rolling me over before withdrawing, and gathering me into his chest. Exhaustion weighs heavy over my body, so much that I'm hardly bothered when both our releases leak down my leg to the sheets.

The way he's holding me to him tells me that he wouldn't care about the mess and would rather stay like this, possibly forever.

Not a bad idea, honestly.

I'd always wondered what my first time would be like, and after hearing stories from others of theirs being less than satisfactory, and boring, I thought mine would be the same.

Yet here I am, boneless and snuggled into a man beautiful enough to be carved from the flesh of angels themselves.

My eyes wander the room, scanning the dark curtains framing the window, the long, solid oak dresser next to what looks like a closet, and the dim light from the hallway that filters in through the bottom of the doorway.

Part of me wonders what it would be like to stay here with him, but the other part of me doesn't want to impose on his life more than I already have.

"What are you thinking?"

I blink, my eyes flicking to his as he searches my face. "So where am I sleeping?"

A smile tugs at his lips, as if we both already know the answer. "You're welcome to sleep here, but if you'd like your own bed, there's several spare rooms."

My stomach flips nervously.

Is it too soon to be sleeping in the same room?

We did sort of already sleep together, so I guess it couldn't hurt right?

I chew the inside of my cheek. "What would you prefer?"

He grins, and the knot in my stomach tightens as he gives me a knowing look. "If it were up to me, you'd sleep in this bed for the rest of your life." I feel the blood drain from my face, and he just laughs with a shrug. "Was that too soon?"

Was it?

Part of me knows my parents would scold me to the ends of the earth for doing all of this with someone out of wedlock, someone I've only known for mere weeks, not to mention that he's my professor.

But I can't help this feeling like I know Seir, that I can trust him, and he's always been there for me when no one else has been.

"Ori," he says, searching my face with his features painted with concern, "say something."

"Don't you think you need to get to know me more before you start making statements like that?"

He chuckles, the sound makes my lungs catch as he gives me a matter-of-fact look. "I've been inside your mind for weeks, Ori. I know your heart, and I've seen your soul in all its beauty. So, no, I don't need to get to know you more."

I blink at him.

The look on his face is serious yet lighthearted, and my mouth drops open just as he flips us until he's hovering over me, looking into my eyes.

"Tell me you don't feel the same," he challenges, keeping his voice low.

I can't deny it. Not when every inch of my skin yearns to feel his, and the absence of his presence is like a gaping hole in my heart.

"I feel it too."

A flicker of emotion crosses his face. "Then it's settled, you sleep here."

This is insane. He's acting like... "So, what, now we're just..."

He raises his brow. "Just what, Ori?"

My heart thunders, and I feel it in my throat as I swallow. "We're just a thing, now?"

My voice is no more than a whisper, and the genuine smile that graces his features sends butterflies through my body.

"Are you asking me if we're an inanimate object now?" I roll my eyes, and he just laughs. "Alright, alright. Do you need a label?"

"I need to know what I am to you."

He searches my face for a long moment, his features turning contemplative and serious before he leans in. His breath skates over my skin, and his hand glides up my side until his fingers graze my jaw. He grips my chin, and his lips brush against mine as he holds my gaze.

"You're mine."

Chapter 23

The next morning, the rumble of thunder echoes in the distance as my eyes flutter open. The room is still cloaked in darkness, with flashes of light from the storm illuminating the space for a heartbeat.

As my eyes adjust to the dark I see the outline of Seir lying beside me, his shadowed face peaceful even given the storm that continues to rumble overhead. The memory of his words from last night makes my heart flutter chaotically.

Finding someone who cares for you is one thing, but Seir is different. Attentive, caring, and fiercely protective, add that to the note of possessiveness I felt from him last night, and I don't think I've ever experienced this kind of all-consuming relationship in my life.

Another loud rumble of thunder sounds overhead, and his eyes flutter open.

"You're already awake," he murmurs, his voice is deep, and thick with sleep as his hand flexes against my hip.

My breath hitches, and the way his blue eyes peer at me from beneath his locks of dark hair sends a shiver through me. Taking that as his cue, he tugs me closer into his hold, wrapping his arms around me tightly.

I glance at the dim light from the digital clock on the dresser and groan, "We're going to be late."

Another flash of light brightens the room as Seir leans in, placing kisses along my shoulder, and up my neck. "Being fashionably late never hurt anyone."

I'm about to argue when he nips at a sensitive spot on the tender area along the side of my neck, and desire pools low in my core.

Despite still being sore from last night, that doesn't stop me from leaning into him, my fingers digging into his skin. His breath catches, and within seconds he's on top of me, guiding my leg around his waist.

Pressing his delicious weight down, the length of him throbs against my already soaked entrance, and he groans into my chest before raising his forehead to mine.

Our breath mingles as he leans in closer, and a creak near the doorway makes him freeze. A click echoes into the stillness of the room as the light flicks on, and my heart skips a beat.

"How many times to I need to remind y—" A deep voice reverberates before stopping abruptly. "Well, well, well, isn't this a surprise."

Seir rolls his eyes, "Do you forget that a closed door means privacy, Vassago?"

Catching sight of the newcomer over Seir's shoulder, my gaze lands on a familiar face—his blonde hair isn't styled now, and he doesn't have glasses on, but here I am staring at the face of my public defender.

He must recognize me too as his bright grey eyes widen, and a grin spreads across his face. "Oh, naughty, naughty, Seir. Fraternizing with your student."

Seir huffs, sliding out from the covers and stalking toward the door fully nude.

"So you two know each other, then?"

Before Seir can shove Vassago out, he's stepped inside, grinning from ear to ear as Seir sighs.

Vassago crosses his arms over his chest, and raises a brow at Seir. "You could say that."

My voice is barely more than a whisper as I try to make heads and tails of the connection between the two men in front of me. "How is it that my public defender just happens to know my professor?"

The two men share a look before Seir sighs again in resignation. "It's less that your public defender knows me, and more that I know someone who could effectively defend you in court and get what we needed."

I blink at him. "You were pulling strings the whole time?"

A slight smile tugs at his lips as he shrugs. "It was appropriate given the circumstances."

"So you were the reason Merrick didn't press charges?"

Vassago shakes his head. "Sorry, but no. Merrick did that of his own accord. Although we did have some evidence that gave him and his legal counsel pause, it was entirely circumstantial, and I doubt it was the driving factor."

So my public defender was really Seir's friend—or roommate? It's still so hard to wrap my head around who Seir really is. It's like one day he was just in my mind, and from there, everything changed.

"You better get going, you two." Vassago sings out, winking at me as he turns toward the door. "Get this beauty some clothes before we both show her a good time."

A low sound rumbles from Seir as he shoves Vassago out the door, turning to give me an apologetic look before picking up my clothes from the floor.

"Not into sharing, I suppose?" I tease, reveling in the way Seir's eyes flash with a mixture of heat and anger.

"Sharing you? Not a chance."

~

By the time we get to campus, my heart is pounding in my throat.

Will people notice we arrived together? Will they say anything?

Could I be expelled if they find out?

Who am I kidding, at a school like this, they'd do worse things if they knew.

I really am playing with fire.

Seir pulls into his parking spot near the side entrance. Before I can reach the door handle, his fingers grasp my jaw, turning my head as his lips crash against mine. Something about the way Seir grips my chin, the borderline desperation and hunger in his kiss, and the absolute wildfire his touch ignites within me fogs my senses.

It's as if everything in my mind goes quiet, singularly focusing on him, here and now. It's intoxicating in the most literal sense.

His hand releases my chin to fist my hair, and I moan as he tugs, taking the opportunity to deepen the kiss. A car horn blares as someone locks their vehicle, and we both pause.

There goes the moment.

"You can go in first. I need to stop by the office," he whispers, searching my eyes with a heated look on his face that tells me if I don't leave this vehicle now, we might not go inside until lunch.

It's not a bad thought.

"Ori..." He warns as if he somehow knows exactly the turn my thoughts made.

"Alright, fine. Sheesh. Forgive a girl for feeling things."

His gaze softens, and I tear my eyes from him, forcefully giving myself the motivation I need to exit the car. Granted, the heat between my legs is indication that I have more than enough motivation to stay.

Climbing out of the car, I freeze when I hear Seir groan. Following his line of sight, I notice the dark, glistening spot on the leather seat. The proof of my own arousal sends a flush to my cheeks, which is only intensified tenfold by the way Seir looks like it's taking every ounce of restraint to not drag me back into the car and fuck me.

Again, an intensely tempting idea.

"I've reconsidered," he growls, surging out of the car with a speed that is borderline inhuman. "Fuck the office. We'll walk together."

I can hardly suppress the giggle as he steps up to my side, the look on his face nothing short of predatory. He mutters something under his breath, but a large SUV pulling into the parking lot revs its engine as it passes by, drowning out other sounds as we walk to the doors.

Our arms brush lightly, sending electricity through my body at the contact before he reaches forward, pulling the door open with his free hand at the small of my back.

I'm once again struck by the small gestures he makes—the ease of which he makes them, almost as if they are second nature, or as easy as breathing.

The genuine smile on his face sends my mind into a nervous haze, and by the time we reach the classroom, I'm blushing for thirty different reasons but all of them revolve around Seir.

He holds the door open, and I breeze past him, focusing my attention on the handful of eyes that turn to us as I walk briskly to my desk beside Rae, who's looking at me with a knowing grin.

I swear she has a sixth sense for this shit.

Settling my bag down alongside the leg of my desk, I return my gaze to the center of the room near the chalkboard to see Seir grasping the book from the middle of his desk just as the door to the room opens once more.

My heart drops as Merrick waltzes through the doorway like he owns the place with a fake smile plastered across his features. Murmurs ripple through the room, with some students turning to look at me nervously.

Like they're waiting for me to snap and attack him again.

My heart stutters in my chest, my lungs seizing as if the oxygen in the air around me has been sucked out, including that which resided in my lungs themselves.

Why is he here? It should be weeks before he's back, right?

Isn't there some protective order stating we can't be around one another?

Merrick walks down the aisle, and my entire body stills as he turns to walk the aisle alongside my desk. I feel my eyes widen in panic, and in my moment of desperation I look at Seir.

There has to be something he can do.

Something.

Anything.

When my eyes find his, he's already looking at me with a heady mixture of concern and barely-contained rage.

He didn't know this was going to happen either.

"Ah. Good morning. I've been assigned to assist with your classes for today, and resume teaching this course from tomorrow on. I'll just be an observer for the day, so don't mind me." Merrick's gravelly voice grates against my nerves as he slowly reaches the front of the room.

Seir's jaw ticks, but that's the only indication of his malcontent before he gives Merrick a tight smile. "Absolutely."

Merrick snatches the booklet from Seir's hand, flipping through it with a hint of disgust. "And where were you in this... thing?" He practically chews the words out, and Seir levels him with a deadpan stare.

"Section Three."

Merrick looks down, flipping through the third section before a smile creeps across his face. The two men lock eyes in what I can only describe as a silent challenge. If I wasn't already creeped out by Merrick, the look he's giving Seir right now would be one for the books.

Merrick's face is a mixture of taunt and triumph, whereas Seir's expression is as if he's imagining stabbing Merrick repeatedly with a toothpick—directly into his eyeballs.

After a long, tense moment, Merrick turns to the class. "Well, I'll let our fearless professor... what did you say your name was again?"

"Harvard."

"Ah, Mr. Harvard, please continue your course."

Seir clicks his teeth, barely masking his disdain as he stares at Merrick. "Everyone should have read through part three. We're going to discuss the testaments in theology that surround demonology."

I'd read most of part three. It spoke of the various texts in different cultures before diving into demons and their cultural significance. I'd read all the way through to the texts dedicated to demons, but I'd stopped before it went into describing the demons themselves.

"Oh, I love this one in particular." The look Merrick gives Seir sends a shiver of nervousness down my spine. It's like he's somehow excited for something, or can't wait to rub something in Seir's face.

Ocean blue eyes flick to mine, and for a moment I'm frozen, pinned in place by the overarching concern whirling behind his irises. Merrick follows his gaze, and before he looks at me, I drop my vision to the floor, watching them in my peripherals.

"Well, Mr. Harvard. Do continue." Merrick sneers, sauntering to the empty chair by the desk.

I don't miss the way anger flashes across Seir's face, his jaw feathering with tension before he clicks his tongue. "Who can tell me then, what is the religious text of islam called?"

Seir's authoritative tone fills the room, and someone near the front raises their hand.

"Is it the Qur'an?"

Seir nods, "Very good. What about Hinduism?"

Silence falls over the class, but when a student tentatively raises their hand in front of me, Seir's lips twitch into a small smile. His eyes meet mine briefly, and my heart flutters before he gestures to the student. "Speak."

"H-hinduism has many texts, but the more prominent is the Vedas."

Seir nods in approval. "Can anyone tell me what other texts are important to Hinduism?"

My hand hardly twitches upward before Seir gestures to me. "Oriana."

The difference between him addressing the other students and myself is stark, and I swallow hard as Merrick's eyes narrow on me.

"The Ramayana, the Mahabharata, the Puranas, the Upanishads and the Bhagavad Gita... to name a few."

Pride flashes across Seir's face as Merrick claps slowly, and my chest tightens.

How the hell am I going to manage staying in this class?

Ignoring Merrick, Seir continues, "Christianity?"

A few hands raise into the air throughout the class, and Seir gestures to a girl in the back right of the classroom. "Speak."

"The Bible!" she announces proudly, and those around her nod in affirmation as Seir tilts his head to the side.

"What variations of the Bible exist?"

"The Old and New Testaments," She recites without a second thought.

Seir nods once. "As you know these are just a handful of texts within various religions. All of which have differences between them. Each describe events which people claimed to have occurred and recounts of historically significant religious moments."

"What about the texts that refers to demons?" Merrick chimes in impatiently as Seir visibly stiffens.

A student to my left raises their hand, and Merrick gestures toward him, "Luke, go ahead."

Luke straightens in his chair and clears his throat nervously. "Outside of historical texts, there are additional works that were created such as the Lemegeton, also known as the Lesser Key of Solomon."

Seir's jaw grinds so tight that it flexes on either side, and even from here I can see the white in his knuckles as he grips the edge of his desk.

"Ah yes, The Lemegeton. Say, Mr. Harvard, what is the content of the Lemegeton, again?" The resolute challenge in Merrick's expression has my stomach turning as I glance between them.

"It is an anonymously written five-grimoire series on demonology."

Seir glares at Merrick, and the clipped edge to his voice doesn't help my uneasiness. Knowing how strong Seir is, he's probably having to restrain himself from actually hurting Merrick in front of an entire class.

Merrick snaps his fingers. "Right, right. Parlor tricks that summon nothing more than dogs to do their masters bidding." He chuckles as Seir's hands turn a rather unnatural hue as his fists flex.

I glance down at the booklet, frowning before glancing between the two men once more.

Why is this bothering him so much?

"Rabid dogs can still bite, Merrick," Seir grinds out, and I flip further into the book. The turning of the pages fills the air as my gaze falls on the descriptions of the Lemegeton.

It describes the manuscript as what many understand to be based on the Testament of Solomon, and how the five books are broken out, listing them by name.

Ars Goetia.

Ars Theurgia-Goetia.

Ars Paulina.

Ars Almadel.

Ars Notoria.

The next page lists the seventy-two various demons in the hierarchy, and as I scan through, some hold familiarity from other ancient texts. The Kings are listed as Bael, Asmodeus, Purson, Vine, Beleth, Paimon, Balam, Zagan, and Belial...

I lazily survey through the list of Dukes, again noting some familiar names. Agares, Dantalion, Amdusias, Vapula, Aym, Bathin, Zepar, Eligos, Gusion, Barbas, Valefor, Vepar, Astaroth, Berith, and

Buné. I continue through the rest of the list before moving to the princes.

The number of princes is far shorter, thankfully.

Ipos, Sitri, Gäap, Stolas, Orobas—

I freeze at the next two names listed with a cold note of dread shooting down my spine.

Prince Vassago.

My gaze flicks to the last name, and though everything inside of me screams in warning, my stomach knots and my palms suddenly grow slick with sweat. It takes everything I have not to react to the name staring back at me.

Prince Seir.

That can't be possible. They're not real.

In a conflicting state of denial and terror, I snap the book shut. I feel eyes turn in my direction, but I can't bring myself to look at the front of the room.

What if he senses my nervousness?

Would he even tell me the truth?

It's obvious he's not human, and though I had convinced myself he was some sort of alien, my mind wars with itself as I fight the realization that the man I spent the night with might actually be one of the princes of Hell. The logical part of me insists that this must be some sort of coincidence, but it's barely convincing.

Chapter 24

The moment class is over, I sling my bag over my shoulder, and haul Rae from the room by her arm.

"Hey! Ori! Not so tight. Sheesh," Rae swats at my hand, wincing at my unintentionally bruising grip as we speed-walk down the hall.

I need space. I need time to think.

My breaths come in shorter as my head feels light.

Oh God, I need air.

Pausing alongside the admin office, near the bulletin board, I glance around to see no sign of Seir before Rae's concerned eyes find mine. "Are you okay?"

I know her question is directed toward Merrick more than it is any sort of revelation I've had, and I shake my head as I gulp down breaths. "No. I need to get away from here."

She nods, scanning the hallway before gesturing to the bulletin board over my shoulder. "What about that?"

I to see a handful of pamphlets pinned to the cork surface, seeing a bunch of after-school church programs listed. One in particular catches my attention, and I twist to fully face the board before pulling the pin from the paper to read through it.

A week-long retreat to reinvest into the community. It's volunteer work—cooking, cleaning, organizing for charities with an all-inclusive stay.

My heart irrationally aches at the thought of being away from Seir for that long, but between him and Merrick, I just need time to think. "I'm going to do it. After last night, and now Merrick being back, I can't deal with this. I need a clear head."

Rae nods from where she reads over my shoulder. "Okay."

"Rae I need you to do me a favor," I say, glancing at her. "I need you to not tell Mr. Harvard what I'm doing."

She frowns. "What? Why? Did something happen? Oh my god, did he hurt you?" The threat in her eyes is real, and I can't help but chuckle as I shake my head.

"No, at least, not that I know of. I just need time away to process, and that includes from him."

She nods, as if she understands the weight of my troubles. Honestly, maybe in some sense she does, especially with how Merrick strode into class like nothing happened.

But, if I tried to tell her that Seir might be not only a demon, but a prince of Hell? Well, regardless of how much she loves me, she might just actually admit me to the hospital.

I know, I would.

I shiver at the memory before steeling my resolve. Keeping my strides purposeful, I make my way to Adam's office, knocking on the wooden door three times.

A chair creaks inside followed by faint footsteps before a creak sounds out, and Adam's figure appears in the slight opening. "Ah, Oriana. How can I help you today?" He opens the door a little bit, gesturing for me to come through.

"I'll meet you in class," Rae says, glancing between us as I nod before following Adam inside.

His room is as bland as ever, with nothing having changed since the last time I was here. When I finally sink into the guest chair, my shoulders sag slightly.

Almost there, Ori.

"I'd like to volunteer for this," I say quietly, sliding the pamphlet across the desk to him.

He barely glances at it for more than a second before nodding. "We can arrange that. It's going to interfere with your OJT hours, though we may be able to consider them depending on what program we get you into."

I nod absently as he types into his laptop, his brows furrowing. "It looks like enrollment ended last night for the volunteers for tomorrow. We will have to wait until next week to get you enrolled."

Panic surges through me as I consider an entire week with Merrick, while grappling with who Seir really is.

"Can you make an exception? Just this once?" He starts to shake his head, but I lean in and give him the closest form of begging that I can muster. "Please, Adam."

He studies me for a long moment before pursing his lips, and clicking his pen a few times. "I'll see if there are some strings I can pull..." His gaze flicks from the screen to me once more, his eyes narrowing, "Is there a reason for this sudden interest in participating in the retreat?"

I shake my head. "Uh, no. I just didn't know it existed until now and don't want to miss out."

His eyes linger as he considers my answer before he nods. "I will see what I can do. See me after class and I should have an answer by then."

A heady mix of hope and relief surges through me, and I breathe easier as I push to my feet.

Just get through the rest of the day, Ori.

That's all we need to do.

Murmuring a word of thanks, I walk to the door and take a step into the hallway, turning toward my second last class of the day.

Just a few more hours.

Classes go by in a blur, and after confirming with Adam that I'm enrolled in the retreat tomorrow morning, I'm lost in thought when Rae hooks her arm around mine, tugging me into the hallway.

"Ori, are you sure about this?" The concern on her face tightens the emotions clogging my throat, but I swallow against it as I nod.

"I'm certain. Can I borrow some clothes, though?"

She wouldn't understand anyways, and it's best if I don't involve her more than I already have. I can't help but wonder if she's in danger because of what I've already divulged.

She grins. "I'm surprised you didn't ask earlier... Are you staying with—"

I shake my head and her mouth snaps shut. "No. If I can crash on your parents couch tonight, I'd appreciate it."

Rae eyes me warily, and I know she wants to ask more, but I'm not in the mood–or place–to explain. She must come to the same conclusion, because she just shrugs and leads me toward the front entrance to campus.

"Ori."

My heart nearly leaps from my chest as Seir's voice sounds out beside me, and my pulse spikes as I turn toward him.

"Hey." I cringe internally at the way my voice cracks.

His piercing blue gaze searches my face, with apprehension and concern etched into his features as he takes a step closer. My body recognizes him, still remembering the way he felt on top of me, and a large part of me wants nothing more than to embrace him, to feel his skin against mine.

But he has too many secrets, and until I get time to think and process, it's dangerous to continue the way we have. Richard's warning blares in my mind once more, and my palms start to sweat.

"Are you alright?" It's hard to know if he's asking because of Merrick, or implying something more, so I just avert my eyes.

If only to stop myself from giving away my nervousness, I nod. "Yeah. I'm okay. I'm going to Rae's tonight to get some clothes and I'll be spending the night there with her family after dinner."

I'm not sure why I feel the need to explain myself on why I'm not coming home with him tonight. Perhaps some part of me doesn't want him to feel rejected, or hurt.

Despite the obvious red flags, I know that I care for him, even regardless of the knowledge that there's a chance he's a demon. But the chance that he could have been manipulating me all this time is a possibility that I can't seem to shake.

For all my bluster about how demons aren't inherently evil beings, when faced with the fact that this clearly supernatural entity could be a demon and one of the princes of hell...

It's all more than my mind can handle right now when added to Merrick's return.

Seir's piercing blue eyes studies me for a long moment before he inclines his head. "Alright, Ori. Just be safe. Call me if you need me."

I swallow and give him a tight smile before Rae tugs on my arm, leading us out the doors. Each step feels like I'm being torn between sprinting back to the perceived safety of Seir, while equally seeking some semblance of normalcy again.

This is going to be a long night.

By the time we're at Rae's parents' house, they've already left for the evening, leaving the two of us to our own devices as I watch Rae rummage through her dresser for clothes I can borrow. Taking another bite of a chicken tender, I tilt my head to the side as she places another pleated skirt on the bed beside me.

"You know Brad's parents invited me to another dinner on Monday."

I raise my brow at her. "Again? Aren't they sick of you by now?"

She laughs, tossing a pair of socks at my head with surprising accuracy. I manage to dodge them with a squeal before throwing them back at her with more force.

"Honestly, they're not bad people. Super involved with the church but they're easy to get along with."

I watch as her features soften, and a slight smile tugs at her lips. "Oh my gosh, Rae."

Her green eyes flick to mine, suddenly filled with worry. "What is it?"

"You love him, don't you?"

She rolls her eyes, but I don't miss the pink flush to her cheeks, and the way she chews the inside of her lip nervously.

"Well... Just make sure you use protection, I guess."

Her eyes bulge and she turns her head toward me. "Pot, meet kettle."

My mouth snaps shut, and she winces slightly. "Sorry. I don't know what happened with you two, but judging by your reaction any time he's brought up, I shouldn't have said that."

"It's fine." My voice is hardly more than a whisper as I shove the rest of the tender into my mouth, chewing slowly.

Rae's eyes linger on me for a moment before she sighs. "Wanna sleep here tonight instead of the couch?"

The look she's giving me is like she can see behind the specially curated mask I've created. As if the years and years of experiences we've had together, the moments we've shared, have allowed her to break past each barrier I've put up until she can see directly into the core of my soul.

I nod, not trusting my voice because of the emotion tightening my chest.

She places the clothes into the bag before flopping onto the bed, grabbing a chicken tender and taking a bite. "Whatever is going on between you two, Ori... just make sure you talk to him rather than shutting him out."

My mouth drops open to protest, but she puts her palm out to silence me. "Just listen to me for a minute, okay? When your parents died, you didn't speak for days—weeks maybe. You hardly ate, barely slept. I listened to you cry yourself to sleep every night, and pretend like nothing happened. Everyone moved on, thinking you were okay, but I knew the truth of it. Even though your parents were cruel and fanatical, you still loved them and that's okay. But it took you years to open up to **me** about that abuse. You never even told me how you felt after they passed, and we went about life as normal as possible."

She sets the empty plate on the end table before taking my hand and tugging me alongside her on the bed. When I'm finally settled in, she reaches up to flick the table lamp off, and holds my hands between us.

"You shut me out until Seir showed up, and then I finally got my best friend—my sister—back." Tears flow from my eyes as she continues. "For the first time in what feels like months—maybe years even—you've gotten some semblance of the old you again. I've seen it, heard it and felt it. I don't want you to lose that just because of a communication issue."

Maybe my fear of the unknown is causing me to react worse than I should, but how can I just ask Seir if he's a fucking demon prince without sounding crazy?

He's just as likely to kill me for knowing who—or what—he really is, and that's not considering how absolutely insane it is to ask that question seriously. Nobody just asks someone if they're a prince of hell because of a possible coincidence with their name.

I nod, knowing she can only hear my hair rustling against the pillow.

"Love you, Ori."

I swallow, my voice wavering as I whisper back, "I love you too, Rae."

Chapter 25

After a week of cleaning, serving in a soup kitchen, washing and folding clothes of the homeless, and endlessly scrubbing the shelter bathrooms, I'm exhausted beyond all reason.

Before I left, Adam confirmed the hours would go toward my OJT, even though the tasks were not similar, they made an exception due to the impact the volunteerism program had on the shelter.

I haven't seen nor heard from Seir the entire week—not that I'd reached out to him to tell him where I was, anyways.

Still, there were nights I'd lay awake, thinking of him in entirely inappropriate ways before crying myself to sleep because of how alone I felt. Other times, I'd remember that he's more than likely one of the more prominent demons in history, and worry that he'd find me anyways like he promised.

Sometimes, in the darkness of my small room, I'd feel his presence around me and search the shadows that flicker in each corner of the room before rolling over to force myself to sleep. Though, I was never able to escape the feeling of being watched no matter how hard I'd try.

A few times, I whispered his name into the dark, only to be answered with a silence that made my soul ache like I've missed every moment with him since I left... since our mental connection was broken.

Every now and again I'd call Rae's cell, and in the week I'd been away, Rae's parents filed an insurance claim for the damage the fire caused, but it would be at least another few months before they received any type of compensation, pending the results of an investigation to rule out fraud.

But now, as my taxi pulls up to Rae's parents' house, I exhale a shaky breath, steeling myself to dive back into my life like nothing is wrong. As if I haven't been quietly dying inside, separated from both my best friend and the man I somehow have tied myself to in such an intimate way that being apart from him feels like the air has been sucked out of the room.

My mind is a jumble of thoughts as I secure my bag over my shoulder, and unlock the front door with the spare key Rae gave me. The door creaks open, and an eerie silence fills the house.

Rae said she'd be home, though her parents went out of town on a work trip, but the lights are all off. An unsettling sense of dread washes over me as I gingerly set my bag down, careful not to make any noise as I slowly creep down the hallway.

When I reach the entrance of Rae's bedroom, I notice the door is half ajar, and in the dim afternoon light, I see a figure hunched over Rae's limp form on the floor.

No.

No, not Rae.

That's when I see the blown out candles and blood surrounding her body before my vision goes red. I reach down between the mattresses for the knife I know she always keeps in her bed and sprint at the intruder crouched mere feet away.

Fuck if I die.

That's my fucking sister.

I don't even know if she's alive, but the amount of blood on her bedroom floor tells me it's unlikely.

I charge at the tall figure's broad back and dark hair comes into view as the stranger starts to stand, turning slightly as I hurl myself onto his back.

My body collides with the intruder's with a grunt, and I thrust the blade into his shoulder. The blade tears through the strangers flesh, and bile rises in my throat at the feeling.

To my surprise, the attack doesn't catch the intruder off guard as he continues to turn, so I rip the blade from his flesh only to drive it in again deeper.

"Ori!" Seir's voice cuts through the chaos as I scream.

Maybe he's here to help, to keep this intruder from killing Rae and I both. Clinging to that hope, I yank the blade from the intruder's flesh once more, recoiling for another strike when a large hand wraps around my wrist.

"Ori, stop!"

The intruder easily shakes the miniscule weapon from my hand, forcing me back against the wall before tilting my head up. My heart skips a beat when I'm staring into piercing blue eyes that look like they hold the weight of the world in them.

"Seir?" My entire body starts to tremble, and my breaths come in short, frantic gasps.

Why is he here?

My gaze drops to Rae's lifeless body, to the deep gaping crimson-stained wound in her chest, and as my limbs shake, a wave of nausea washes over me as I shove Seir away with force, doubling over to empty the contents of my stomach onto the floor.

Seir's hands pull my hair back as I continue to heave, and by the time I'm done vomiting, my body is numb, with my legs struggling to keep me upright.

"We need to leave," his voice is quiet but firm as he reaches for my arm.

Shock flashes across his face as I wrench my arm from his grip. "I'm not going anywhere with you."

"Ori, we don't have time—"

"You killed my best friend!" I shout, pounding my fists against his chest and shoving him back. He doesn't fight back or move to stop me, but the conflict in his eyes tells me everything I need to know—he is responsible for her death.

In some way, I know it.

"I will kill you myself. I don't care if you're a fucking demon. Hell, kill me for all I care. You'll have to or else I will kill you for what you've done."

Hurt flashes across his features, giving me all the confirmation I need before I scream as loud as I can. If I'm going to die here, I might as well alert people to our deaths.

"Oriana, please. Trust me. This was going to happen regardless—"

"Don't try to pretend you didn't do this when I found you at the scene of the fucking crime, Seir!" My voice is shrill, and his jaw feathers before anger flashes across his face.

He surges toward me, his grasp nearly bruising as he pins me to the wall. "If you would let me explain—"

I scream loud again, cutting him off abruptly before he can gaslight me further, and he covers my mouth with his hand. Rage and desperation coat my veins as I bite down hard. My teeth tearing into the flesh of his hand as he recoils.

Taking the opportunity, I bring my knee up into his groin before shoving him backward. He stumbles with a grunt, tripping on a rogue mascara tube on the floor, sending his foot outward, and before he can recover I twist, sprinting from the room as fast as I can.

"Oriana!"

Seir's voice bellows from the room, but I'm already at the front door, yanking it open and bolting down the steps. Adrenaline and desperation mixed with the bitter taste of betrayal push me forward as I cut left at the sidewalk.

I need to get away. This was my fault.

I involved her with him, and she's dead because of me.

A car engine rumbles to life behind me, but I don't dare turn around. I can't afford to lose momentum as I race toward the busy main road.

I need to get somewhere safe. Somewhere he won't be able to find me.

Hearing the engine in the distance get louder, my stomach churns and a fresh wave of adrenaline pumps through me, propelling me faster around the final corner. The crowded street lined with rows of shops comes into view, and once I reach the clusters of pedestrians I slow down.

Weaving around groups, dodging dogs and strollers, I duck into a pedestrian alley, slipping into a narrow crevice along the wall. Hidden from view of any cars on the street, I squeeze myself closer to the wall as an engine passes by, and I hold my breath, praying it wasn't him.

Images of Rae's body flutter into my mind, and my hands shake uncontrollably as I wrap my arms around my body. A sob escapes me, and I slide down the wall until my knees hit my chest.

She's gone.

My best fucking friend—my sister—is gone.

My fucking sister—

Tears flow freely down my face, and I bury my head into my knees, wrapping my arms around them as if they're the only thing holding me together. There is no place left for me.

I have no one now, nothing.

Everyone around me dies, and it's all my fault. Had I never involved her in this by telling her about Seir, she might still be alive.

A stabbing pain radiates through my chest as I shudder, unable to stop the way my breath hitches with each sob, and tears stream down my face.

Footsteps approach in the alley, and my breath catches with the fear that he's somehow found me. My head whips toward the sound only to see a group of teenagers as they walk past, their eyes wide like they just saw a ghost.

When in all actuality, they're witnessing everything within me shattering, falling to pieces in an alley because the man I gave myself to murdered my best friend.

I couldn't care less about how I look right now, I'm certain I'm a blubbering mess that anyone would want to avoid, and based off recent events, they should avoid me. I do nothing but bring death to those I've ever cared about. What happened today is proof.

Maybe this is a sign that I shouldn't devote my life to helping others sort through their problems.

How could I, when even my own problems can't be worked through?

Hell, I fell for a fucking demon.

Oh, God.

The pain in my chest feels like it could tear me apart as my sobs wrack through my body, and I mourn the loss of not only Rae, but the man I had given a piece of my soul to. Another car passes on the main street, and dread coils in my gut.

For a moment I consider calling the police to report Rae's murder, but the memory of being found by Merrick's mutilated corpse flashes into my mind, and I know I can't do that.

The police would just assume it was me, that I snapped, and as much as I deserve to be alone, the thought of being medicated again like that turns my empty stomach. It would either be that or prison.

Besides, Rae wouldn't want me to throw myself into a life of jail or medication.

So I resign myself to running—to finding a refuge where I can push away all that I hold dear to me, which isn't much anymore, and disappear forever.

My exhausted mind races, and I consider my options. Most shelters are too close, and I can't return to the one I worked with the school on in case Seir has connections there.

I settle on the one place where I'm certain no one will look for me, and resolve sinks into my veins, seeping into the marrow of my bones as I push shakily to my feet.

There's a nunnery in the next town over, which I have just enough money to get there but nothing more.

That should be fine considering I don't plan to leave.

Chapter 26

The forest surrounding the nunnery is thick, and as the taxi brought me further from town, I questioned if I'd done the right thing. Somewhere around the halfway mark, the thought crossed my mind that the driver could easily take me somewhere unknown, and leave me stranded or worse, but thankfully his intentions were harmless.

I don't know whether I'm relieved or disappointed about that.

It's like some part of me knows I deserve punishment, as if I should be reprimanded for abandoning my best friend when she needed me most, and falling–hard–for a demon.

My parents are probably cursing me from their graves right now.

The taxi turns onto a long, winding driveway, and soon a cluster of log buildings that resemble large cabins come into view. A few nuns are scattered around the area, some walking into various buildings, one speaks to someone in a simple white uniform, and another shows another person in white how to pull a root vegetable from the garden.

I'm assuming the white uniform is for volunteers, as I spot one person in white sweeping dirt from the house.

"Here you are," the driver says gruffly as he pulls up to the nearest building, and I hand him the rest of my cash before sliding out of the back seat.

The nunnery is large but humble, with a wide garden between the buildings that looks well tended despite a few bare spots. I wrap my arms around myself, and hesitantly make my way to the nearest building. Inside is a small meeting area with two waiting chairs that look hardly used, and my gaze falls to a nun sitting behind the front desk.

She smiles warmly as I step closer, and the corners of her brown eyes crinkle. "Hello, how can we help you today?"

"I'm here to live-in volunteer, actually."

If she's surprised, she doesn't show it as she nods, pulling a piece of paper from a folder, and setting it on the desk between us. "Fill this out as much as you can and then return it back. Once you're done we'll get you settled in."

I nod, stepping closer to take the paper and a pen from the holder next to it. Filling out my personal information, my stomach turns as my mind wanders, randomly returning to Rae over and over again. I allow the pain through—the knowledge that I'm responsible and that I will never see her again.

The twinkle of mischief in her eyes, her curiosity, her deep understanding, even without me having to say anything at all. Rae was wise beyond her years, and she deserved to live. A tear streams down my cheek, and I sign the bottom of the page.

No. If anyone should be dead right now, it's me.

Passing the completed paperwork to the woman before me, she scans it over with a nod. "Great. I'm Sister Marianne. It's good to meet you... let's get you situated then." She smiles warmly at me, but I don't miss the way her eyes linger on the tear-stained trail on my skin before she leads us through the buildings.

"This is the living quarters," she says, gesturing to a room full of cots. "We share a room here between all of us. Personal belongings remain near or under your bed." The area is sparse, with hardly any items near or around them save a book or glasses case. Phone chargers plugged into the wall tell me they're not entirely disconnected from the world.

She leads me into the next room which is filled with long tables and countless chairs that line them. It reminds me of a cafeteria, and my assumption is reaffirmed by the long wall of countertop with a bustling kitchen behind it. The scent of various foods wafts over, and my mouth waters as the sound of sizzling reaches my ears.

She guides me through the various buildings, and introduces me as the newcomer to all the other live-in volunteers and nuns. Some ask how long I'm staying for, or what brought me to them, but they all quickly pick up on my reluctance to talk about it, and thankfully drop the subject.

By the time she's shown me around the various buildings, and introduced me to the other volunteers, the sun has long since set. Exhaustion mixed with a deep-seated ache in my chest has settled in, and I want nothing more than to disappear into the darkness dancing along the walls as the oil lamps flicker.

"Well, you better get some rest," Nancy, another volunteer I met earlier says, gesturing to an empty cot along the wall. "They like to throw more on you early on. Weeds out the ones here for the wrong reasons."

I huff a dry laugh, waving dismissively before throwing myself into bed. "They can try to weed me out all they want."

Chapter 27

I thought finding sleep was hard after my parents died, but nothing could have prepared me for trying to turn my mind off after seeing the man I care so deeply about after he murdered my best friend.

No matter if my eyes are open or closed, I still see her blood pooled on the ground. Seir's body hunched over her, caught in the act. The way he didn't even flinch after I stabbed him not once, but twice. How easily he disarmed me.

Rae didn't stand a chance.

Everything I thought about the nature of demons went out the window the moment I saw him standing over her.

No, there is true evil in this world, and Rae was the victim of it.

Tears spring to my eyes, and my chest tightens as I feel the sob clawing its way out. The way my heart aches is nothing in comparison to the pain she probably felt.

How could I have left her alone?

She was fucking alone.

My sister.

My breath hitches as tears stream down my face, the sudden sound of my ragged inhale is louder than intended, and I roll over to face the rest of the room.

Part of me doesn't care if the others hear me cry, but the other part of me wants to hide away where Seir can't find me, and making any sound or existing loud in any capacity is too risky.

Because even though I had no tracks to cover, I still feel like he could be right on my tail. My eyes flick to the corners of the room, remembering how he suddenly appeared at the foot of my bed as anxiety swells within me.

What if he did appear?

Would he try to kill me?

Could I kill him like I promised I would?

My insides twist painfully, and I blow out a breath.

It takes everything I have not to focus on the shadows in the corner of the room as if they could be hiding him within them.

No. I can't keep thinking of what-ifs or dwelling on the past. Nothing can change what has already happened, but I sure as hell can focus on what is to come.

I owe that much to Rae.

Chapter 28

Nancy was right about one thing, they really do throw everything and the kitchen sink at you in the beginning.

My first morning was spent sprinting from the main house to the barn, and then to scrub the wash house and clean the bathrooms. The amount of laundry needing to be done was a pile taller than me, and the nunnery doesn't have a washer or dryer, so everything is washed by hand before being hung on clothing lines.

By the time I've finished quarter of the pile, my fingers are shriveled like raisins, numb from rubbing clothes along the brass washboard to clean them.

I'm in the middle of loading the wet sheets and dresses into a basket when Sister Marianne walks into the room with three strangers in tow.

"This is the laundry room–" she gestures into the rather unimpressive area, a slight flush reaching her cheeks when she spots me near the basin and starts to wring her hands together. "Ah. Oriana. Good evening. Sorry to bother you, Marcus, Tony and David requested a tour of our nunnery."

I glance at the three middle-aged men, and can't help the suspicion that washes over me. "Sorry, Sister Marianne. Do you need me to leave?"

Marianne shakes her head, waving her hand in dismissal. "Not at all child, we still have three more buildings to tour and those clothes aren't going to hang themselves."

The man in the back chuckles before turning out the door with the others following suit, and I find myself a little more on edge than I had been previously.

What if they work for Seir?

Could he have found me already?

A shiver runs down my spine, and I haul the heavy basket to the courtyard, casting cursory glances over my shoulder every few steps.

In fact, it's not until the last heavy, hand-wrung bedsheet is hung that I finally manage to take a deep breath. The air fills my lungs, and even though my body recognizes this as a peaceful moment, no sense of relief comes from it.

No, if anything it's been days, weeks even since I've felt some semblance of normalcy, or miniscule drop of respite. My mind wanders as I walk across the courtyard to the main house, and the rumble of an engine catches my attention.

Slowly, a white car with tinted windows comes into view beyond the main house, creeping past the driveway before turning toward the highway. The only road out of here is that way, and I watch the car moves eerily slow before it starts to turn.

That must have been those three guys doing the tour.

Judging by what I've seen so far, this place rarely gets visitors, so for me to be volunteering and then three curious male visitors suddenly decide to do a tour...

My stomach twists, and I quicken my pace to the house as the engine fades into the distance.

They'll be a concern for another day.

Within seconds, I slip through the doorway and hurry into the living quarters, feeling my anxiety spike until I reach my cot, nestled between two other live-in volunteers who are already settled in for the night.

The dry, warm breeze from the window glides across my skin, and I suppress a shiver before climbing into bed. Memories of Seir resurface, and conflict wars in my mind once more as I pull the blanket up to my chest.

My eyes slide shut as tears well beneath them.

How could I be so stupid?

So blind to the truth?

My chest tightens, and I swallow hard.

I know that I can't keep letting him dominate my thoughts like this, but it feels impossible to avoid when the silence allows torrents of memories through like an open door.

No matter how busy I stay, it seems impossible to drown him out.

Someone turns over nearby, and my hair stands on end at the back of my neck. I squeeze my eyes shut and take a deep breath.

One day at a time, Ori.

Just take it one day at a time.

My breaths even out, and I slowly sink deeper into the cot until my mind goes blissfully blank.

Chapter 29

There's a rhythmic thumping in my ear, slowly growing louder with each passing second as a gentle feeling of contentment eases over my body.

The blanket over my chest feels heavy, and the log cabin holds a familiar scent as I peel my eyes open a sliver. The dark is imposing, but my heart stutters when I vaguely recognize Seir's chest as it rises and falls with my head resting against his skin.

My eyes flutter shut, still fully invested in returning to sleep as I squeeze myself into him more, feeling his arm tighten around me in response.

I don't know how long I've been lying there against him when sleep is finally about to claim me. My mind jolts to the present and my eyes snap open only to find my face nestled into my pillow, and I'm intertwined into my bedsheets as if I'd been tossing and turning in my sleep.

It was just a dream, Ori.

It's fine.

He doesn't know where you are.

For the remainder of the night, I lay there awake and restless, smelling the remnants of his woodsy cologne while trying to convince myself it wasn't real until the sun rises.

Chapter 30

After a long week of physical labor from nine to five, I'd spent the rest of my time keeping busy. Being stagnant or allowing my mind to wander freely meant it would find a way back to him... back to her... and I can't allow that to happen.

Not during the day, anyways.

But nighttime is always a different story.

When the volunteers and nuns were asleep in their beds around me, the little privacy left my mind unoccupied, and my silent tears were usually the last thing I remembered before exhaustion finally claimed me.

Every night I'd be haunted by dreams of Seir.

Some nights I'd dream that I sense him close, opening my eyes to see him approaching the bed. Even though I was terrified, I'd remind myself it's not real, and that no one knows where I am. Most nights he'd crawl into my cot, and pull me into his arms.

I'd remain awake in my dream as long as possible, reminding myself that he's a killer. Whenever I'd make concessions for him, I'd remind myself of Rae. Whenever I'd feel that burning desire or heat in my body, I'd remind myself, he's a murderer.

But every night, I'd fall asleep in his arms in my dreams only to wake up to a mess of my bed, and an exhaustion that feels like it could crumble the very foundation of my existence.

On the morning of the sixth day, I'm carrying linens to the washing room when Mother Janine, the Abbess of the nunnery, approaches me.

She wrings her hands, a habit I've noticed in a few of the older women here, so while normally it would have, it doesn't strike me as part of nerves at all or if she's going to approach a difficult topic.

"Oriana, we need some herbs and groceries from town. Would you mind accompanying Holly on a trip?"

"Absolutely, Mother." I reply, spotting Holly near the corner of the nearest building, and she gives me a wave as I smooth my skirts. "We'll head there now, then."

Janine gives me a curt nod before taking over washing, and I quickly make my way to Holly.

"Hello Oriana," Holly gives me a soft smile.

"Hi." I attempt a smile in return, but it feels more like I'm baring my teeth than anything.

She blinks, and an awkward silence ensues as she turns, and leads the way to the truck at the edge of the driveway. The ride to town is short but quiet. Even with the radio on, I fight to keep my mind from wandering, focusing instead on the road and scenery around us to keep myself in the present.

Because the moment I let myself think about either of them, I'll break down again.

When we finally reach the small town, my thoughts drift to Seir, wondering if he has even tried to look for me, or if he got the hint and left me alone to my own devices.

Alone is just how I need to be.

Holly pulls into a semi crowded parking lot and parks between another truck and a van before turning off the engine.

"Alright. Let's get what we need and be on our way then," she sighs, pushing her door open and sliding out of the truck.

When we get near the front doors, I grab a small hand basket and follow Holly around, collecting items from the list as we slowly walk down the aisles.

By the time she's halfway through the list, the basket is full, and she chuckles before heading to the front to get a small cart, murmuring that the list seemed shorter before we started shopping.

After checking out, we have five full bags of various items we can't grow or source at the nunnery. We're mere feet from the entrance when Holly sighs loudly.

"I forgot to get milk and butter. Here," she says, passing me her two bags, and I manage to shift them all into my grip. "I'll run to grab them, if you can bring these to the truck."

"Sure," I say, noting the twinge of pain in my wrists from the bags biting into them, and the tension in my arms grows as I struggle to hold up all five.

I hurry to the truck, if only to put the bags down faster, and with each consecutive step, the weight of the bags feels like it's doubled. When I finally reach the driver's side door, I breathe a sigh of relief as I squeeze between the vehicles to rest the bags on the ground, flexing my hands as the pain and tension subsides.

I'm so focused on the pain in my limbs that I don't notice the quiet click and rumble of a door sliding open until a hand covers my mouth, dragging me backward.

The grocery bags rustle as my feet kick, and my shouts are muffled by the hand tightly clamped over my lips. Strong arms pull me in as I thrash and flail, trying with everything I have to break free. Within seconds, I'm pulled against a hard body, and a healthy mixture of panic and adrenaline course through my veins as the door slides shut with a click.

My captors are tall, masked, and one is much heavier set than the others. The car pulls out of the parking lot, and I catch a glimpse of the top of Holly's head through the window as I try to scream. The captor covering my mouth pinches my nose with his other hand, cutting off both sound and my air supply.

He doesn't let go even after I stop making noise, and I thrash again in desperation, lightheaded from the lack of oxygen. After what feels like an eternity, my head throbs before he finally releases my nose and I suck in a deep breath.

One of my captors reaches over my head and I freeze.

Is this it? Is he going to choke me to death?

The hand covering my mouth is quickly replaced by a cloth, and my captor fastens the material at the back of my head. The knot catches my hair, ripping it from my scalp and I whimper at the sharp sting.

"Bitch almost got us caught," The large man growls, scratching the length of his neck as the man behind me rolls me onto my side, pulling my arms behind my back.

Panic rises in my chest as he grips one of my wrists, and I start to thrash again, managing to kick the large man in chaotic movements in a shitty attempt to break free.

The large man leans forward to jerk me to my side before backhanding me across the face. Stars explode in my vision, and my head snaps to the side. My cheek tingles and burns, and I choke back the sob that rises in my throat.

What the fuck do they want from me?

"Easy," one of them warns, "We don't know what the boss wants from her. If we fuck up his plans, we're as dead as she is."

Dead? Someone wants me dead? Could it be Seir?

Has he finally decided to cut ties with me? To free himself of loose ends and those who know he's a demon?

"Guess the bitch doesn't want to die with the way she froze up," the large man bellows, laughing as the others join in and the vehicle comes to a stop.

*What do I do? What **can** I do?*

I swallow hard and after a long while the vehicle comes to a stop. The musty cloth in my mouth makes bile rise in my throat as the door clicks open. My nerves are on alert right now, and my fight-or-flight response is on the cusp of being triggered as I'm dragged out of the vehicle by my restrained arms.

The warehouse they're dragging me toward has one open entrance, with its rusted door propped open by a brick. My chest tightens, and my palms grow slick with sweat as they drag me inside. Behind me, I hear someone kick the brick out before the door slams shut.

I'm so fucked.

"Boss, we got her," the large man bellows, his voice sound echoing through the near-empty warehouse.

I guess they're not concerned about being heard, so screaming for help isn't an option. Glancing at the large man, and the third, quieter masked man beside him, I notice the pistol at their hips, and I swallow nervously.

Fighting my way out is not going to work, then. Not that I would have won anyways.

Footsteps draw my attention, and my stomach churns with dread as I brace myself, expecting to see Seir. But as the figure approaches, my breath catches when it's Merrick taking confident strides until he's mere feet before me.

Oh, God help me.

His grin widens when he sees the recognition on my face. "Oriana Sharpe," he says, his familiar gravelly voice echoes into the warehouse. "How lovely of you to show your face again."

Two more men step into view on either side of him.

Six total.

There's no way I can escape six armed men.

I'm so beyond fucked.

"I'm glad we got to you before your boyfriend did. I have to say, fraternizing with your professor is bad enough, but a demon?" He tuts, shaking his head disapprovingly. "I have to say I hoped better of you."

Hoped better of me? I nearly killed him.

Okay, Seir almost killed him once.

Still.

Merrick must notice the flush in my cheeks as he sneers. "Godfrey," he says, tilting his head toward me, "remove her gag. No one will hear her anyway."

I swallow hard as the cloth around my mouth loosens before falling to the ground, and a cold wave of dread washes over me.

Godfrey?

As in...

My wide eyes track the movement of the man who removed my gag as he returns to the circle of men surrounding me. Merrick laughs as he takes in my reaction, but I can hardly pay attention as I stare at the masked man in disbelief.

There's no way this could be Brad's dad.

"She's already starting to connect the dots," Merrick says cheerfully. "Always been a bright one, just like her parents. You can remove your masks. She won't be leaving here alive to tell the story, and I want to see her face when she realizes."

Godfrey removes his mask, as the others follow suit, and I gasp, blinking at each of them with wide eyes.

They're all board members of DCC.

My attention slides to Merrick, who looks giddy with excitement as I realize his little corrupt boy band is made up of the most powerful men in the city.

"What the fuck do you want from me, Merrick?"

Anger flashes across his face, and the large man–Godfrey–steps forward, backhanding me hard. A metallic tang fills my mouth as my head snaps to the side. Tears stream down my face drawn out by the searing pain where my teeth tore through the soft skin of my cheek.

I lean forward, crimson saliva streaming from my mouth as Merrick chuckles, looking at the large man beside me. "A little unorthodox, but I'll allow it—if only as minor payback for the stunt you pulled at my house." His face darkens as he studies me. "How did you manage to overpower me, anyway?"

I opt to stay quiet. Even if Seir's a fucking demon, I won't out him like that, especially not to this maniac.

When I don't answer, Merrick shrugs. "Oh well. Not like it will matter soon enough. With Rae-Ann out of the picture, courtesy of Godfrey, and the Sharpes no longer in play, dare I say that our control over this city has been very lucrative."

Did he just imply what I think he did?

My entire body freezes as I look between Merrick and Godfrey with shock, outrage and denial flooding my veins.

It can't be.

Merrick's grin widens. "Go ahead, Oriana. Ask your question. I can see you have one."

Pain radiates from the cut in my mouth as I force out the words. "Rae's death, was you?" My attention locks onto Godfrey, who only raises a brow in amusement, glancing at Merrick as if waiting for approval to respond.

Merrick gives him a nod, as if he's more than excited to indulge my question.

"That low-born whore was never a good match for my son," Godfrey sneers. "A godless family filled with sin could never be worthy of such a prized man."

Anger surges through me, and I rear back, my head brushing the hard body of the man behind me. "She was my friend!" I shout, ignoring the pain in my mouth. "She was my sister!" Crimson spittle flies from my lips, and my gaze is drawn to Merrick as he laughs.

"Yes, yes, and she was in the way," Godfrey says, his upper lip curling in disgust.

If Godfrey killed her, that means Seir...

Seir was fucking innocent, and I blamed him solely because he's a demon.

Regret, guilt and shame, like a thick blanket of sorrow weigh heavy on my shoulders. I know there's nothing I can do to take back what I said to him—especially not now—when this warehouse will become my tomb.

Merrick takes two steps forward, stopping inches from where I stand, still restrained by one of the other men. His voice is cold and haunting as he searches my face. "She was in the way, just like your parents, and now, just like you."

Just like my parents?

"My parents were in a car acc–" Humor flashes across his features as my jaw clenches. "You murdered my parents too?"

He grins. "Another courtesy of Godfrey."

I glare at the asshole responsible for the death of my entire family, spitting blood in his direction. It falls short, landing on his shoe. "Go to hell, asshole."

Before I can react, Merrick drives his fist into my stomach. The air is forced from my lungs, and pain radiates through my core as I double over, only being held upright by the man behind me.

Merrick steps back with a triumphant smile as I gasp for breath.

"Hell is real, dear Oriana. And you? You are going to be given one last chance at redemption." He punches me again, this time with more force. My body reacts instantly to the sharp pain radiating along my ribs, heaving the contents of my stomach to the ground with some of it splattering onto Merrick's shoes.

"When we complete the ritual and take your life today, you will be resurrected in His name. You will fight for His army against the forces of Hell. That will be your ultimate sacrifice for divinity."

The ritual?

My mind wanders back to the few classes we'd had before I met Seir, where our entire class was about to learn about soul binding and soul claiming rituals.

My eyes grow wide, and even through the shallow, pained breaths I manage to suck in, his words cut through the haze. Seir's statement from our visit to see Vince echoes once more in my mind, but this time, I finally understand what he meant.

Between Seir and these men, I know who the real demons are, and it's not the prince of Hell.

The men around me move into a patterned position that I painfully recognize, each man placing a candle on the ground and lighting it. Merrick watches them eagerly before placing his own down, then draws some sort of symbol around me that connects to each candle.

"This will be your last chance to achieve that which you were created to achieve, Oriana. Your final opportunity to gain access to an eternity of bliss. When you are reborn from the eternal darkness, you will be reunited with your dear friend. That doesn't sound too bad, does it?"

Reborn with Rae from eternal darkness? These guys must be fucking insane.

Voices murmur around me, chanting in a language I don't recognize as the flames from the candles burn impossibly higher. Merrick's excitement is palpable as he reaches behind him, and when his hand comes back into view with a dagger in his grip, ice-cold dread washes over me.

My gaze flicks between him and weapon, and I squirm in an attempt to put distance between us, but I'm held firmly in place. My heart races, and my struggle only seems to please Merrick more as a his malicious grin spreads even more wide.

"With this sacrifice, I give unto thee another Holy Warrior for your divine army, Lord!" Merrick bellows, raising the weapon high. The tip of the blade is aimed directly at my chest as I squeeze my eyes shut, waiting for the inevitable pain.

Waiting for him to drive the blade into my heart, and end my suffering once and for all.

I'm so sorry, Seir...

Chapter 31

But the pain never comes.

The sound of gargling fills the air, and the grip on my arms goes slack as my eyes flutter open.

Merrick's bulging eyes look like they could pop out of his skull with how wide they are. His face is a deep shade of red, almost purple, as he claws at his neck. In my peripherals, the other men have the same desperate look, and I'm certain if I turn around, the others behind me would mirror it.

That's when I notice that the hairs on the back of my neck are standing straight. I recognize the shiver down my spine, the sudden rush of oxygen as I suck in a breath that feels like my first in weeks, filling my starved lungs, and breathing life back into my soul.

Merrick's head looks like it has doubled in size, and he drops to his knees as the figure approaching behind him comes into view.

Seir.

Relief washes over me as he strides closer. His black suit is unbuttoned halfway down his broad chest, his normally styled hair is tousled, and he looks relieved, as if he'd raced fate to get here. His movements are predatory and deliberate as he steps alongside Merrick, like a hunter to his prey. But his rage-filled gaze never leaves me.

Whatever he was doing to Merrick ceases as he suddenly gasps for breath, coughing and sputtering while the others still choke around us.

Seir's features soften as his ocean-blue eyes search mine, and they drop to my mouth as his jaw feathers. "Ori, you're bleeding." The apprehension in his voice is clear, as if uncertain whether I still think of him as evil. "Are you hurt?"

A tear slips down my cheek, and he tracks the movement as I nod slightly.

"You abomination!" Merrick spits as Seir waves his hand in the air. Simultaneously, the other men drop to the ground, lifeless. I glance at each, seeing blood streaming from their swollen eyes, nose and mouth. Their faces are unrecognizable, like black and purple overblown balloons from where they lie in heaps.

"How unoriginal," Seir mutters, rolling his eyes before moving to step closer. He pauses with his palms between us as if calming a scared animal. "May I remove your restraints?" he asks gently, as if him being behind me or being close to me is more of a threat.

After what I just witnessed, it wouldn't matter anyways. If Seir wanted me dead, I'd have already been dead long ago.

I swallow, and he watches my throat bob before his lips press into a thin line.

How do I tell him that I was wrong? How do I admit my own faults when they were so hurtful?

I nod, glancing at Merrick, who remains held in place by some invisible force as Seir steps to my side, and I feel him gently untie the rope binding my wrists together.

As the restraints fall to the ground with a soft thud, I feel his gentle touch graze the raw and more than likely bruised skin. The moment his touch disappears, I bring my arms forward and gingerly rub my wrists.

Each breath still comes in pained, and I'm nearly certain Merrick broke a rib earlier.

"You and your kind will burn in Hell for all eternity. You will not win this war, demon." Merrick snarls as Seir steps forward, tilting his head to scan him head to toe.

"We have been at this for far longer than you have lived, and your false empire is crumbling," Seir replies, and a content, victorious grin grows on his face as he takes another step closer. "I will sleep soundly, breathe easily and revel in the knowledge that you won't be here to contribute to its failure any longer."

Seir recoils his fist and hurls it into Merrick's face. The sickening crunch of bone snapping fills the air as blood streams down his chin and neck from the bones in his cheek that jut through his skin.

The damage Seir caused with a single punch sends a wave of an emotion over me that I can't quite place.

No wonder Merrick was an inch from death when I let him in.

I watch as Merrick begins to choke once more, strangulated by an unseen force as Seir tilts his head. He watches with cold fascination as Merrick struggles, gulping like a fish, his mouth opening and closing as his face turns from red to purple.

Merrick's limbs suddenly bend in unnatural ways, snapping with a crunch that I'll remember for the rest of my life, and his mouth drops open with a silent scream. His clothes turn crimson as blood seeps through the fabric, pouring from deep wounds that suddenly appear all over his body.

This level of torture sends bile into my throat, and even though I hate Merrick, I'm not sure that I can continue to watch.

My gaze averts to Seir, and I tenderly wrap my arms around my torso, wincing when pain jolts in my chest. He must notice because in the same instant, Merrick's body drops to the ground, unmoving.

His expression is conflicted, a mix of apprehension and something else I can't quite place as his mouth drops open to speak.

"I want to apologize," I blurt out. Surprise flickers across his face, but he stays silent, so I press on. "When I connected the dots as to who you were, I panicked. I thought distance to be the best course of action, but when I returned and saw you standing over Rae's body...”

My hand covers my mouth as the memory flicks through my mind. The pain in my ribs jostles as I shudder, and tears flow freely as Seir takes a tentative step closer.

“Ori, I never would have—” He starts to say, but stops abruptly as I nod.

“I know, and I should have known that then. I should have realized. I'm so fucking sorry for what I said, Seir. I'll understand if you don't forgive me, I don't deserve forgiveness.”

My body trembles violently as I choke back a sob, but Seir just shakes his head.

“Forgiveness would imply you did anything wrong, Oriana. You did not wrong me.”

“I stabbed you repeatedly with a pocket knife.”

He chuckles. “It was basically the equivalent of a papercut.”

“I told you that I'd kill you and called you a demon.”

My eyes widen as he shrugs. “I am widely considered a demon, and who knows, maybe you will kill me someday.” A car engine passes by outside, and we pause until it fades into the distance before sharing a look.

“We should go. My car is outside.” Seir says, extending his hand in my direction.

I glance at the heaps of bodies around us before I slide my hand into his. “How did you know they brought me here?”

A smile tugs at his lips. “I pride myself on being able to find things that are lost, you know. I knew you were grieving, but when you ran away, I struggled to keep my distance.” He leads us toward the side entrance, opening the door as the sunlight hits my eyes. My short breaths still make me lightheaded, and I lean on Seir's strength to keep myself upright.

“I knew who was responsible for Rae's death and that the fire at your house was no accident, but I worried that while you were on the run, they would try to get to you, so I made a point of following them. When they showed up at the nunnery, I knew they were going to make an attempt to abduct you, I just needed to be able to be there when they did. Though, I did not anticipate that Merrick would send the entire board of DCC to do it, so I was delayed because the men I was following were not the ones tasked with kidnapping you."

He holds the car door open and moves to help me climb in as I turn, blinking up at him, "Wait... you knew where I was the whole time?"

His lips twitch as he leans in close, and his dark hair tickles my forehead. "I told you, Oriana Sharpe. I wasn't going to let anything happen to you. I keep my promises."

Part of me starts to wonder if my dreams were really dreams at all, but his nose brushes mine, and my heart flutters as my mind goes blank.

It's not until a car engine approaches that he pulls back, and I take my cue to gingerly slide into the passenger seat.

But there's still one thing bothering me, though. Merrick and the others didn't have any abilities, nor did they act very angelic. Could it be that they were just regular people?

I track Seir's movement as he strides to the drivers side, shifting it in gear before I find my voice. "If you're a demon, what did that make Merrick, Godfrey and the others?"

"Misguided souls. Corrupt, iniquitous, and nefarious individuals tainted by the will of a far more malicious being than you or I have ever met."

I frown. "But you follow Samael?"

Seir nods, turning the wheel as he merges onto the highway. "He's dangerous, Ori. Trust me when I say, he is a force to be reckoned with, in addition to having a brilliant mind. If there is any reason we win this war, it will be because of him."

My brows pinch together even further. "So they were going to kill me to become a holy warrior in their war?"

Seir's jaw flexes. "I'm surprised they told you that much. Usually, they just complete the ritual and force the soul to undergo transition without explanation. None of us know what happens to those they murder or where they go. None save for Samael himself." His ocean-blue eyes flick to mine before returning to the road ahead as he weaves between vehicles at top speeds. "It's above our pay grade to know that level of detail."

I swallow. "But we know that Rae is wherever they go after transitioning?"

Seir nods. "People like Merrick and their secret societies have spent years molding families, cities, and countries into the perfect test subjects. They create religious trauma by influencing people with control over others, and then they farm souls for their army. The more the soul believes they're going to redemption, the more likely they'll be malleable in the war ahead. It's why the work we do to counteract their influence is so important."

My mind races to really absorb the information, and the rest of the drive is quiet, allowing me to gather my thoughts before he slows down, yielding onto empty streets.

Knowing that I could have fallen to the same fate as Rae sends a nervous chill down my spine, and I swallow hard when I consider the fact that they tricked Seir into following the wrong people.

My voice is hardly more than a whisper as I glance at the prince of hell responsible for saving my life. "Thank you, Seir."

"I don't know why you're thanking me, Ori. I told you already, I am selfish. I am greedy. And when it comes to you, there is not a single place in this world you could go that I would not find you."

My chest tightens as he turns into the long driveway toward his house. The guards in front of the gate give him a nod before it opens, and the realization finally sinks in.

"So you really command legions?"

His lips twitch, and he glances at me with amusement. "Twenty-six of them, yes."

I wasn't expecting so much honesty. It makes me want to ask more questions.

"And they live with you?"

He bursts out laughing, shaking his head. "No, there's only a handful here with me, and Vassago."

I frown. "Where are the rest?"

Seir's piercing ocean blue eyes snap to mine, and he grins as I roll my eyes. "Right. That's probably confidential."

"Quick learner."

I release a long, drawn-out sigh, wincing when it radiates pain through my chest, and I watch trees pass by as Seir brings us to a stop in front of his house.

"So, what now?"

He turns off the engine and leans back, tilting his head to study my face. "Well, with Merrick and the DCC board out of the picture, I assume the school will fill their places and move on. So, for now, I think things will be looking up in the near future."

He eases closer, leaning over the center console, his palm cupping my cheek. "Would I be overstepping by asking you to stay with me?"

My pulse quickens as his thumb glides along my cheek. "If you'll have me, I would love to stay." His face lights up, but a lingering doubt tugs at the back of my mind. "But, should I just stay in school like nothing happened?"

He pauses, searching my face and his brows furrow. "I'd understand if you didn't want to, but if you still wish to go into counseling, I see no reason for you to drop out or change course."

If I want to stay in counseling.

Chewing the inside of my lip, my gaze drops between us. "I'm still passionate about it. I just don't know if that's where I belong anymore. How can I continue on when I know so much?"

When I look into Seir's eyes, his confidence feels almost contagious.

"You'll make an impact just by being there for those at risk of being manipulated by corrupt people or people with power. You'll help far more people than you realize."

The way he says it is like he already knows the outcome, and sees everything good that will come from it.

That's when the realization hits me, and I stare at him wide-eyed. "You can see projections of the future."

The answering twinkle in his eye as he grins at me is the only answer I get before he leans in, brushing his lips against mine, and my entire body is suddenly alight.

"Now, let's get those broken ribs fixed."

Epilogue

"Oriana!"

I turn toward Vince's voice as he saunters down the hallway, adjusting his backpack with a genuine smile plastered on his face. It's hard to believe five years have passed since we first met—the little boy who still seemed so happy even in the face of the abuse he endured.

It's a testament of his will, really.

And Seir's sincerity.

By the time Vince reaches me, I ruffle his blonde hair loosely with my hand as he swats me away.

"How was school, kiddo?"

He groans, giving me a dramatic frown. "It was good, but I hate math."

I can't fight the smile that tugs on my lips. "Yeah, math does suck." I agree with a nod, and we both turn toward the front doors.

"Are we going to Seir's house?!" He asks excitedly, and I nod as he squirms victoriously.

A few months ago, Seir saw Vince's situation take a turn for the worst, so we discussed various ways to be there for him, before deciding to use the after-school program to our advantage. The abuse still got worse, but we've been able to give him some solace while Seir looks for the best way to rescue him.

According to what Vince's future looks like, we have only mere months before his father and uncle end his life, but Seir is confident we'll intervene fully before then.

Still, it has me on edge though.

The urge to just steal him away is strong, but Seir has unprompted and firmly reminded me multiple times that it would do more harm than good.

I guess there must be some future he's seen where it happens.

Whoops.

Maybe it's more than a strong urge.

We walk past the front doors to Seir's awaiting vehicle, the engine purring as the dark tinted windows leave no hints as to who is inside.

I know it's him, though.

The way my body urges me to get into the car, to be as close to him as possible. Even in a crowded room, I'd still be able to find him with my eyes closed.

Vince sprints to the car, his backpack bouncing as he flings open the door and crawls inside, squealing Seir's name. My chest tightens at the sight of them grinning at one another as Vince rambles on about his day.

It's an odd feeling, having grown up catholic only to find yourself on the side of demons as an adult.

I shut the door as Vince clicks his seatbelt in place, and unease washes over me as my eyes scan the parking lot. It's not until my gaze lands on a mirage of faces near the bus stop, halting on one that makes my heart nearly stutter out of my chest.

Merrick.

The bus pulls forward, obscuring Merrick from view, and when it finally drives past, he's gone.

I swallow hard.

The knowledge that they're murdering innocent people to force them to join some holy war is horrifying enough, but the thought that Merrick could still be out there, alive and corrupting others...

I slide into the passenger seat, my eyes darting nervously toward the bus stop.

"What is it?" Seir asks, his brows pinched together in a mixture of confusion and worry.

Shaking my head, I tear my eyes from the crowd of students and teachers to look at him.

"It's nothing. I must be imagining things."

His attention lingers on me before he scans the crowd, and only when he's certain there's no one there does he put the car into drive.

I don't know what the future holds for us, or if we'll ever truly be rid of Merrick and the others, but I do know we'll save as many innocent lives as we can.

With everything at stake in this war, we have no other choice.

This has to be enough.

Acknowledgements

I have to first, again, say a huge thank you to Amanda Dumky for the insanely gorgeous cover. I will forever appreciate your immense talent more than you will ever possibly know.

A huge thank you to my husband, who supports all my chaotic hobbies, endeavors and passions without a second thought. I love you to the moon and back. In all the romances I write, there's always so many layers of the devotion and undying love that you surround me with that inspires these connections, and I will never take that for granted.

Thank you to my street team for being so supportive, hyping me up even when I was lost in the sauce, and always bringing excitement to my life. You are all beautiful humans and I cannot tell you how thankful I am to have you all in my life.

Lastly, much like with my Unbroken series, thank you to all the readers who decided to give this new series a chance. I can't promise it's the most well written, or well written at all... but I, as with many authors, put a piece of myself into my work, and taking the time to read it... well that may be the best gift of all.

It's just my hope that you enjoyed it, even if only for a moment before you move on to your next adventure.

Other works by Aella C Grey

The Unbroken Series
Shadows of Dusk (Unbroken Book 1)
Light of Dawn (Unbroken Book 2)

More Prince of Hell standalone novels coming soon...